"You've moved how many times?" the school counselor asked me after my mother left. She'd squinted at my information card where I'd run out of room listing all my previous schools.

I told her I'd lost count on the moves. It was somewhere between eleven and fourteen, but I couldn't remember the exact number. My mother had a lot of job transfers. And a lot of middle-of-the-night urges to move. I didn't tell her that last part.

The counselor pointed at the space on the card where you're supposed to put your father's name. I'd written "nonexistent."

"What does that mean?" she had asked, tapping my answer with her pencil eraser.

I shrugged my shoulders and answered with just a hint of sarcasm. "It means my father doesn't exist."

She sighed heavily. Kids like me present so many problems. We don't even have enough social training to keep from being rude. She wrote me a pass and sent me back to class, but I knew what she was thinking. If I had a father, I wouldn't have such a smart mouth. I wouldn't be *At Risk*.

Angels
on the
Roof

A Novel by
Martha Moore

Published by
Bantam Doubleday Dell Books for Young Readers
a division of
Random House, Inc.
1540 Broadway
New York, New York 10036

Visit us on the Web! www.randomhouse.com

Educators and librarians, for a variety of teaching tools, visit us at
www.randomhouse.com/teachers

ISBN: 0-440-22806-9

RL: 5.3

Reprinted by arrangement with Delacorte Press

Printed in the United States of America

November 1999

10 9 8 7 6 5 4

OPM

*For Cindy, Jacki, and Danny
and in memory of Kenny and
Marilynne*

Acknowledgments

A SPECIAL THANKS TO: JACKI, WHO LISTENED EVERY SATURDAY morning; so many wonderful friends who encouraged, read manuscripts, and bought enough of my books to start a small bookstore; Jeannine, who said, "You need to be writing. Come get my computer and keep it as long as you want, forever if you need to"; that first little group at Denny's (Hannah, F.J., and Susan), who helped me believe in myself; Howard, Michael, and Peter, who put up with microwave dinners, my strange working hours, and papers all over the house; my fellow teachers, who kept track of my glasses and my grade book; and all of my students over the years who have given me their voices. Finally, Karen Wojtyla, my editor, who helped so much to make a dream come true—thank you.

Chapter One

W HEN I WALKED IN THE DOOR FROM SCHOOL, my mother was standing on the coffee table. She had a row of thumbtacks between her teeth, and a stack of old calendars at her feet. Half of the living room was already covered with pictures, and she was working on the second half. It was just the beginning. Pretty soon Georgia O'Keeffe would completely take over our lives.

In case you don't know, Georgia O'Keeffe was an artist who painted pictures of giant flowers and cow bones. She painted a few other things, too, such as red hills and black doors. That was a long time ago. Women could barely even vote.

Now she's a Fun Ed course at the community center: "Georgia O'Keeffe's World, $55." The description in the catalog says, "When this artist looked at a flower, it became her whole world." That's the part that caught my mother's attention. She works at Roses and Wreaths Florist. All day long she wraps green floral tape around flower stems.

1

"When I see a carnation, I feel tired," she told me. "I'd like to look at a flower and see the world turn beautiful." After that, she took three twenties out of our grocery money and signed up for the course.

Over the years my mother's had a lot of phases: Ceramics, Sand Candles, Designing with Buttons, and Denim Art, just to name a few. I figured Georgia O'Keeffe would pass and we wouldn't even have to have a garage sale to get rid of her.

In the meantime, my mother couldn't get enough. Every day when she came home from work, she sat in the recliner with her lap full of art books. She read out loud whether I was listening or not, spouting off a million loony ideas about an artist who was born over a hundred years ago. I mean, she'd be a skeleton by now.

"Georgia O'Keeffe spent years painting pictures of this one door," my mother said. She held up a book with a photograph of a painting. "It took her ten years to get it right."

What's to get right? I'd like to know. The door was a black rectangle painted on a tan wall. It was something I could have done when I was five, and I'm not artistic at all.

"The feeling was the thing," my mother answered. "Not the door itself." She stopped and thought. "A door is like, is like, a kind of opening, it's . . ." She bit her bottom lip and thought.

My mother was flipping out. I was even more sure of it when she showed me the photograph of Georgia

O'Keeffe sitting in the backseat of a car. The woman was holding a piece of Swiss cheese up to her eye.

"She's looking at the sky," my mother reported, as if taking the cheese out of a sandwich and looking through one of its holes was a perfectly ordinary thing to do. "It gives a different perspective." Right. To me, Georgia O'Keeffe sounded like a person who needed to get a life. My mother was inspired.

That's when she covered the walls in our living room and kitchen with calendar pages: giant bones flying through the sky like dinosaur birds, poppies as big as hubcaps, and hills that could have been the wrinkled bottoms of newborn puppies. I had to eat breakfast looking at the stuff. Then she pulled her hair into a bun and dressed in black, just like Georgia O'Keeffe did almost a century ago.

This behavior caused lots of problems for me. For example, the day she came for a parent conference at school. She walked into the counseling office wearing a long black skirt with elastic in the waist and a black jacket. She'd stuck this huge white gardenia in her hair, right up front like a headlight. I could have died.

The counselor had called us both in to discuss some test scores. The school couldn't figure out how someone on the *At Risk* list could score so high. You can be labeled *At Risk* if (A) you're from a broken home, (B) you fail two subjects, or (C) you're on the free lunch program. That's me, *A* and *C*.

I'm smart—everybody says so, especially the tests that measure your intelligence—but I can't always remember things. Take the word *egregious,* for example. I'd forgotten it on the vocabulary test that morning, but remembered it at my locker fifteen minutes later.

"You've moved how many times?" The school counselor asked me after my mother left. She'd squinted at my information card where I'd run out of room listing all my previous schools.

I told her I'd lost count on the moves. It was somewhere between eleven and fourteen, but I couldn't remember the exact number. My mother had a lot of job transfers. And a lot of middle-of-the-night urges to move. I didn't tell her that last part.

The counselor pointed at the space on the card where you're supposed to put your father's name. I'd written "nonexistent."

"What does that mean?" she had asked, tapping my answer with her pencil eraser.

I shrugged my shoulders and answered with just a hint of sarcasm. "It means my father doesn't exist."

She sighed heavily. Kids like me present so many problems. We don't even have enough social training to keep from being rude. She wrote me a pass and sent me back to class, but I knew what she was thinking. If I had a father, I wouldn't have such a smart mouth. I wouldn't be *At Risk*.

It was on Valentine's Day when I was ten that I asked my mother to tell me the truth about him. We were drinking strawberry sodas and eating strawberry shortcake for breakfast. Everything was red, even the cake and whipped cream. She had a ring of red around her lips from the soda, and her teeth were pink. I was mad.

She'd wiped her lips with a napkin. "Is my tongue red?" she'd asked, sticking it out at me. I didn't smile. It wasn't funny at the time and it's still not.

She fiddled with her hair, wrapping it around and around her finger. "The thing is, your father disappeared." She cleared her throat like she does when she's nervous.

I didn't say anything.

"Let me put it this way." She cleared her throat again.

"Remember when you were five and you tried to dig that hole to China? Every single morning you got a spoon out of the kitchen drawer and headed to the backyard. You thought if you tried just one more time, you'd look down and see people riding bicycles on the other side of the earth."

"What does that have to do with my father?"

She shrugged. "You were just looking for something that couldn't be found, I guess."

"You used to say he was the North Wind." I stabbed toothpicks into my strawberry cake while I talked. "You said he blew in one night and left me on the windowsill. You must have thought I was really stupid."

"I thought you were too young to understand. I just wanted to do what was best, honest."

"So what was his name?"

She considered my question, thinking slowly, as if she were searching through a giant book of names in her head.

"Steven, I guess," she said finally.

"Do you even have a picture of him?"

She shook her head. "Shelby, he's gone. I don't want to talk about it anymore."

I jabbed the rest of the box of toothpicks into my cake, covering the whole top.

My father had slid off the face of the earth like a piece of Jell-O. Or he'd exploded into a million pieces like a fireworks display on the Fourth of July. He'd been here, that much was perfectly clear. I was proof.

The next day I went to school and announced that my father was an astronaut. "He wears a silver space suit and he's hooked to a long cord so he won't get lost in space," I said. That night my mother got a call from the teacher.

"Could Shelby's father come for career day?" she wanted to know. "We haven't had an astronaut before." My mother said he wouldn't be coming down for a long time.

Now that I'm just about grown, I don't even think about him anymore. Neither does my mother. She's got her boyfriend, John D., to worry about. The problem is he wants a woman who cooks real macaroni and cheese, not the box kind, and who irons his shirts in front of *Love Connection* on TV. My mother is definitely not it, not to mention her Georgia O'Keeffe obsession. John D. never did like some dead artist getting all the attention.

The only thing good about him is that he fixes our car for free. It certainly wouldn't break my heart to see him go. The scary thing is what always happens next. I'll come home from school and find a U-Haul trailer parked at our door.

As far as my mother's boyfriends go, some I've liked—the one before John D., for example. He actually read magazines that didn't start with the word *Auto* or *Cycle*. And once, when he saw me reading *Of Mice and Men,* he checked it out of the library and read it himself. For three days we talked about the ending, how terrible it was.

It didn't last, though. Right after they broke up, my mother woke me up in the middle of the night and told me to get packed. It was two A.M. when we headed out and she didn't even know for sure where we were going. That's when we moved into this apartment. We've been here nearly a whole school year, the longest we've stayed anywhere.

I told Roo, my best friend, that I didn't want to move again, even if it meant putting up with John D. forever. I wouldn't have to do that, though. It wasn't long before Georgia O'Keeffe completely pushed him over the edge.

At first he thought my mother's new hobby was cute. He even bought a cow skull at an estate auction, painted it red, white, and blue, and gave it to her, saying it was an O'Keeffe original. She did not think it was funny. She stayed home even more, reading tons of books about the artist, her life, her letters, everything.

"Do you know why Georgia O'Keeffe painted flowers that covered the entire canvas?" my mother asked one day.

I had no idea.

"You wouldn't stop and look at a regular-size flower, that's why."

I didn't want to look. Neither did John D.

After a while, when he thought he was losing her completely, he got desperate. He started buying us presents. He bought my mother a jewelry box that played "Somewhere, My Love," and me a T-shirt with a huge picture of Cinderella in a fat pink dress feeding some squirrels. My mother doesn't wear jewelry, and me, well, let's just say John D. doesn't know the first thing about me.

Finally, one night my mother was looking at her art slides. I had just walked through the living room on my way to the refrigerator when there was a knock at the door. A pounding, actually.

"Shelby, would you go see who it is?" she asked, knowing perfectly well who it was.

I walked to the door and looked through the peephole.

"John D.," I whispered.

She set her jaw. "Well, let him in, I guess."

I unhooked the chain locks and opened the door.

"Hi," he said, bringing his arm from behind his back, where he'd been hiding two clay pots of red plastic tulips, one for me and one for my mother.

I took both pots and set them on her stack of obituaries. She cuts them out of newspapers to give her inspiration when she designs flower arrangements at work.

"We're looking at slides if you care to stay." My mother's voice was as cold as a frozen TV dinner.

Of course, he cared to. He plopped on the sofa next to me, smelling like he always did, a mixture of chewing tobacco and lime aftershave.

My mother went on with her slides just like he wasn't even there. *"Starlight Night,"* she announced, like it was a contestant in a beauty pageant. She clicked off the overhead light and clicked on the projector light. The painting appeared on a sheet she'd hung on the wall across from us.

It was nice in a way, even though it wasn't anything like stars, or any kind of night I'd ever seen. It was exactly like someone had cut little square windows out of the sky. That way the stars could shine through. It was just the opposite of how I'd always thought. You wouldn't expect to find anything behind the sky.

"Look at that trash," John D. blurted. "You call that art? My dog could do that." I'd felt the same way before, but the way he said it was mean.

My mother's body tightened. She spoke carefully, spacing out her words, making sure none of them knocked together. "John D., as I have tried to explain before, this artist didn't try to paint the world accurately, as you might see it, for example. She painted the way she felt when she looked at the world. That way her paintings would be totally hers. They'd be unique."

"That's a bunch of hogwash, Zoe." John D. said my mother's name as if it rhymed with *Joey*, instead of *doe*, as she preferred. She'd told him a thousand times how to say it.

I turned on the lights.

"That's the problem with the world today," John D. complained. "People go to seeing things any way they want, even if it's not right." He spit on his finger and shined a dull spot on the toe of his boot.

"Why'd you come here?" my mother asked. I was wondering the same thing.

The veins in his neck stuck out like he'd been doing push-ups. "I was hoping I could talk some sense into you." He walked toward her and put his arms around her. "You need me, little girl. I know you better than you know yourself."

People have always described my mother as tiny and cute. In those magazine tests where you measure your wrist to see if you're small-, medium-, or large-boned, she always comes out small. She even wears petite pantyhose. Me, I'm not quite queen-size, but I'm between medium and large on the bones. I wouldn't dare stand on the coffee table. Still, even though she's small, she's strong. She pushed him away.

"You'll have to go now, John D." She wasn't going to argue with him, and I was glad.

I stood and walked to the door. I opened it and held it open. He started to say something; then he shrugged and walked out.

I hoped my mother could finally be happy. What I wanted to do was finish ninth grade in one place.

At first I decided what might keep us from moving again would be a house. Having a furnished apartment makes it too easy to pick up and move. You don't get attached to someone else's carpet or sofa.

"Talk to Roo's mother," I begged one night after supper. Mrs. LaGrone is a realtor. I knew she could get us a good deal on a house. I read aloud ads published in the *Shopper*: "Cute 2 bdrm with fenced backyard. A great fixer-upper for the creative person." And "Heaven on Earth: 2 bdrm with carport and large picture window; needs TLC." My mother wasn't satisfied.

"I'm talking about really moving this time, Shelby. Totally away from here. Besides, we could never afford a house in this city." She pulled the pins from the back of her hair and shook it free. "Georgia O'Keeffe moved clear across the country, from New York to a tiny town in Texas. It was a turning point in her life."

"Number one," I said, "we've had turning points. Too many of them. Number two, you're too hung up on this Georgia O'Keeffe thing. She was insane, if you ask me."

My mother frowned. "She's just a symbol. That's all."

"A symbol without any kids," I argued. "A symbol who wandered around in the desert looking for animal bones. She didn't have anyone else to think about. You do."

A few days later, I was sitting on the floor cutting a toga out of an old sheet for our Latin club banquet.

I'd just gotten the neck hole cut out when my mother walked into the living room and stood at the window.

"The sky was one of the reasons she moved away," she said. "Georgia O'Keeffe loved blue, you know. It's something that will always last." She stared out the window like there really was something to see. "I want to go someplace where there's lots of blue, Shelby. Where something lasts forever."

It's true; the sky around here, what you can see of it, is not that blue, even in the mornings. It's got a coat of grime covering it like hair spray on the bathroom mirror. But it's the sky I've gotten used to. I like it just fine.

In the mornings, when I look out the window in my bedroom, I see bricks, dark red bricks. I like things that don't change.

"I'm tired of sirens," my mother continued. "I'm tired of layers and layers of highways with cars stacked all the way to heaven." She walked to the sofa, sat down, and scooted to the corner, staring at the blank television screen. "I'm tired of not being able to see the end of anything."

I slipped the toga over my head. "I can see the end of something—the school year. I intend to stay exactly where I am."

My mother drew her knees up under her and leaned her head on her arms. "After Georgia O'Keeffe moved to Texas, she went to New Mexico. That's the place she really found herself."

I turned to face her. "You don't need to find yourself! I'll tell you who you are. You're the mother of a teenage daughter who is about to walk in front of a crowd of her peers wearing nothing but a sheet and a laurel wreath on her head. I could use a little help, for a change. Would you hand me that cord off the drapes?"

She reached behind her, pulled the cord off, and handed it to me. I tied it around my waist and stood there. I looked exactly like a person wearing a sheet and drapery cord.

"You've got some loose strings," she said, handing me the scissors from the coffee table. Then she added, "Anyway, you're deliberately missing the whole point about what I've been trying to say."

I glared at her. "I'd just like to know what the point is. Things are fine. Leave them alone. For once."

"That's the main thing that can't happen, Shelby."

I slammed the scissors down on the table. "You always do this to me! You're wrong this time! I'm not going anywhere! Except to my room!"

When I got there, I slammed the door and put on my recording of "Night on Bald Mountain." Then I called Roo.

"She's out of control," I told her. "If I don't do something, I'll be living in an adobe hut in the middle of nowhere. She'll have me digging for the vertebrae of small nocturnal desert mammals."

Roo was silent on the other end of the phone. She's taking Intro to Psychology I, and I knew she was trying to think of the right thing to say.

"Calm down, Shelb," she said finally. "I'll get the name of my mother's gynecologist. It's probably a midlife thing. I saw it on *60 Minutes*."

"She's not that old," I answered, wishing something that simple would work. "She's not exactly midlife."

Roo thought. "Maybe she wants to move all the time because there's something she needs to let go of."

"Maybe so," I said. But the problem is, when my mother lets go, she always takes me with her.

Chapter Two

"So how's your mom?" roo asked me the next day at school.

"Moody. Impulsive. Her normal self. At breakfast she didn't say anything about moving, though."

"Good." Roo leaned against her locker. She folded her arms across her T-shirt. it's great to be a human bean stretched across the front, along with a huge green bean. The thing had cost her twenty-nine can labels and a fifty-word essay on the nutritional value of green vegetables.

I sat down on the floor next to the wall and waited for her to get her books. "Roo, you know I can't move again. I'm already a candidate for the Dysfunctional Family Poster Child." Outside I was joking, but inside I wasn't. Fear crept up my body and settled in my throat. The last thing I wanted to do was cry at school.

Roo opened her locker. She already had it decorated for Valentine's Day. Tiny streamers of hearts and miniature red balloons the size of Ping-Pong balls hung from the ceiling.

15

At Christmas she was the only person in the school with a real tree in her locker. She'd even rigged up lights that came on when you opened the door. Practically the whole school came by to look, until she got caught. The next day the principal made an announcement. "No trees allowed in lockers." He had signs posted all over the building.

Roo said it was worth it. Next year she was going to have a real snowman. She'd already drawn up plans in her industrial arts class. There'd be a small ice chest with a Plexiglas top so that you could see inside, sort of like a museum exhibit. The snowman would be six inches tall, with little peppercorn eyes and a knit hat made out of a sock.

"I'm just doing my part to humanize this institution," she'd told me. "There are three thousand students. Each one has a six-digit ID number and an ethnic code letter. At least now, I'm the girl with the Christmas tree in her locker."

"Here," she said, reaching in the back corner behind a wad of papers. "It was supposed to be for Valentine's Day." She handed me a stuffed toy parrot holding a heart in its beak. "You could use some cheering up."

The yellow feathers on top of his head spiked up in a funny tuft. LaRue LaGrone's about the best friend anybody could have, even if her real name does sound like something on a billboard.

Roo finished loading her books into her backpack. "Stay with us next time. I mean it. My mother's pretty weird too. But we don't move around all the time."

We headed down the hall toward my locker. Roo had her hands in her pockets, her clear vinyl backpack on her shoulders. She was wearing yellow sneakers and baggy blue jeans. Her hair is totally out of control. Curls stick out like loose springs all over her head and her mother's always pushing them down and buying her straighteners. It doesn't do any good. Roo likes the natural look.

Unlike Roo's locker, mine is totally organized. Everything is in order by period number and subject. I even have it color-coded: for example, yellow for physical science, green for Latin. I pulled out my English book and a blue spiral notebook.

The hall was getting crowded as we approached the end of the freshman corridor. Ms. P. stood outside her door reading, as usual. Teachers are supposed to stand in the hall between classes, watching for fights and PDAs, which is official school language for "public displays of affection."

Ms. P. has read seventy-five books during hall duty over the last thirty years, or at least that's what everybody says. If you want to kiss goodbye, you do it by her door. She'll have her nose in something like *War and Peace*.

Roo and I walked in and she nodded, barely glancing over her reading glasses at us.

When the tardy bell rang, she walked in with her head down, still reading her book. After she finished the page she was on, she set it down and picked up a giant poster that was lying facedown on her desk. She turned it around and held the picture up to the class. I couldn't believe my eyes.

"Students, can anyone tell me what this is?"

"Pelvis with Moon," I whispered across the aisle to Roo.

"Shelby? Would you say that so the whole class can hear, please?" Ms. P. waited.

I felt fifty eyeballs burning into me.

"Shelby?"

"I think it's called . . ." I cleared my throat. *"Pelvis with Moon,"* I blurted.

Some guys at the back of the room hooted, and I looked down at my desk.

"Shelby!" Ms. P. exclaimed. "I'm quite impressed!" I felt even worse.

"And the artist, please?"

I mumbled, "Georgia O'Keeffe, I think." Of course, I knew who the artist was and I knew the painting. I see it every day on the wall next to our refrigerator.

The picture looks like a pair of giant wings made out of bone. The thing fills up nearly all the space in the painting, and it flies across the sky, which is a perfectly O'Keeffe thing to do. A pale white moon, the size of a fifty-cent piece, rises above it. That's all there is to it, and it's one of my mother's favorites, one of her flakiest calendar pages.

"How many of you have actually seen a bone hanging in the sky?" Ms. P. looked at the class.

Nobody had.

She picked up a piece of purple chalk. Facing the chalkboard with her back to us, she started at the bottom, drawing a huge letter *A* that stretched all the way to the top of the board.

We watched her rear end jiggle like a water balloon as she followed the *A* with a giant *N*, then a *G*. Finally, she stepped back so that we could see.

The words ANGEL BONES covered the board.

"What does this," she said, dramatically gesturing to the board with a yardstick, "have to do with—this?"

She reached for the worn-out copy of a book sitting on the corner of her desk and waved it in the air.

The entire class groaned. Georgia O'Keeffe was bad enough, but we were sick to death of *Moby-Dick*.

"Can anyone tell me what *angel bones* has to do with the book *Moby-Dick*?"

Roo's hand shot into the air. "Angels have to do with eternity, and *Moby-Dick* is never going to end." She crossed her arms in front of the green bean on her shirt and smiled.

Reginald Blair sits in front of me. He was putting jumbo paper clips on top of his ears. When he got six clips on each ear, he raised his hand.

"Yes, Reginald?" Ms. P. ignored the clips that stuck out like miniature antennas.

"Ms. Pletsinger, do you know how many angels can sit on the end of a paper clip?"

Ms. P.'s eyes widened. "An interesting view of the metaphysical world—that is, if you view angels as being infinitesimal. Do you, Reginald?"

He squirmed in his seat. *Infinitesimal* was definitely over his head.

Ms. P. paused a while longer before she continued. "On the other hand, angels sometimes lumber through the air like flying volcanoes, at least according to John Milton."

She went on to explain how this Milton guy described the whole thing in a poem of only ten thousand lines and how he was blind when he did it. He'd made his wife copy down every word that came out of his mouth, like it was the word of God or something.

Pretty soon Ms. P. got through with Milton and his giant angels and got going on *Moby-Dick* again. She reminded us how Ahab got his leg bone snapped off by the great white whale, how he had to hobble along on a peg. She told us how mad he got, how he wanted revenge, and how he was so determined to find the whale that he carved a map on his wooden leg.

"Ahab keeps chasing the whale even though it's destroying him." She slapped her stick on Reginald's desk and he jumped to attention. "The man's already lost one leg in the battle. What else is he willing to lose?"

She paused and walked back up to the front. Then she began to read to us, tapping the linoleum with her yardstick to make it sound like Ahab's peg leg hitting the deck: ". . . every stroke . . . *tap tap* . . . of his dead limb . . . *tap tap* . . . sounded like a coffin-tap." *Tap . . . tap . . . tap*. She moved to the middle of the room.

"How much hope does Ahab have?" she questioned. "Class? How much hope?"

"None," we all chanted obediently. She smiled and walked to the table under the window where Sophocles swam around and around in his bowl. She shook a few specks from his food box and faced us again.

"Where will Ahab's one-eyed cyclopean view lead him, class?" She paced across the front of the room again, tapping her stick with every step.

Of course, we all knew exactly where it would lead him. She'd told us a thousand times: the same place it led all degenerates, into a whirlpool of destruction. Ahab had carved a map into his own wooden leg, and he would still wind up lost.

"What about the angel bones?" Reginald spoke up. He'd taken off the clips and the tops of his ears were red and creased like they'd been folded into fans.

"Oh, yes, the angel bones." Ms. P. tapped her stick at the words on the board. "I almost forgot. Back to the angel bones, class. Chapter 104, page 380."

Everyone groaned.

The story was, according to Herman Melville, the author of *Moby-Dick*, that in 1842, slaves on a plantation found some gigantic bones buried in a creek bed. They thought for sure they'd found the bones of a fallen angel. Later, though, some scientists in England or somewhere proved them wrong.

"These are not the bones of an angel," the professors reported. "They're the bones of a whale."

"Why do you think Mr. Melville inserted this small detail into his book?" Ms. P. clicked her fingernails on the edge of Sophocles' bowl and waited.

"He had only 56,981 details about the whale and he was trying to get in the *Guinness Book of World Records*?" It was Reginald again.

We all laughed in agreement. We had heard enough about whales to last us a lifetime.

"Shelby?" Ms. P. walked toward me with her yardstick. "Why do you think Melville included angel bones in a book about whales?"

I didn't know. The man was sick. He would have made a good partner for Georgia O'Keeffe.

"Shelby?" Ms. P. was waiting.

You wouldn't expect to find whale bones buried among cotton rows. You wouldn't expect to find angel bones either. But I agreed with the slaves. The earth would be a dangerous place for angels to fly.

Finally, I gave her the one answer every English teacher loves, the answer that fits everything.

"It's a kind of irony, I guess." I was right. It worked.

Her eyes lit up and she went on to discuss the types: irony of situation, verbal irony, and dramatic irony. To me, they're all the same. What you expect is not what you get. Just like life.

On the way home on the school bus, Roo sat beside me folding foil gum wrappers into tiny strips. She's making some kind of recycling project for art class.

"Do you think Ahab was insane?" I asked.

"Please, do we have to talk about *Moby-Dick* again?" She grimaced. "Melville made everything so complicated. I could have told the whole story in three sentences. Man gets hurt by whale. Man chases whale. Man drowns. The end."

"You left out Ishmael. He's stuck on the same boat."

"So?"

"It's me, Roo. Don't you get it? My mother keeps running around everywhere, moving us every time I get comfortable. I'm just like Ishmael. Stuck."

"It's not exactly like your mother's going to sign up to work on a whaling ship."

"I know, but it scares me."

Roo turned to face me. "It's just a story, Shelby. Get a grip."

I couldn't. All I could think about was what happens at the end of the book. The ship goes down with Ahab and all the crew. Everybody's drowned except one person, Ishmael. He's left hanging on to a coffin, all alone in the middle of a great big sea.

Chapter Three

Valentine's day passed. So did march. During all that time, my mother didn't say a word about moving. Maybe it was because her job at the florist shop was going pretty well. For one thing, she got a bonus for designing the best funeral spray of the month. All her years of reading obituaries were finally paying off; she was developing more feeling for the flowers. Plus she used a lot of glitter on the ribbons. People seem to really like that.

Roo said my mother was probably settling down because of her hormones. They were getting in line somehow. Whatever it was, we were in one place. I began to relax.

Then one morning at breakfast, she started up again. "I'm still thinking about New Mexico," she said.

The next thing she did was show me the dumbest photograph in the world: a shriveled-up old lady sitting on top of an adobe house staring into nowhere. You could see the sky behind her. It was

Georgia O'Keeffe, of course. Normal people that age are grandmothers. They don't sit on roofs.

I pushed my cereal bowl away and sat back in my chair. "For the hundredth time, I'm not going to New Mexico."

She totally ignored me. "Everybody there has adobe houses with nice flat roofs. We could join one of those star-watching clubs. And New Mexico's full of artists. They mostly sit around painting, making pottery, and drinking cappuccino."

She chattered on and on, not even noticing that I was shaking my head.

"Of course, I could still work with flowers, only in New Mexico they'd be exotic, I'm sure. I wouldn't be making any pink wrist corsages for school proms. It'd be something like . . ." She couldn't think of anything exotic. She propped her elbows on the table and rested her chin in her hands.

I knew how to get to her. "I'll move in with Roo," I said. Then I added the part that would really sting. "They have a *functional* family."

I knew the statistics. We'd definitely be the other kind: single mom with a string of used boyfriends, non-homeowner, and an *At Risk* daughter who was once a sock girl. Being a sock girl means you get called into the principal's office because someone turns you in for looking like a thrift store reject. It happened when I was in the fourth grade.

"We have a little gift for you," the principal had said, reaching into the bottom drawer of her filing cabinet. She was smiling like one of those cats in a Walt

Disney movie as she watched me and two other kids open our packages of new white socks. I dropped mine into a mailbox when I walked home that afternoon.

It's not like we never have money. My mother just hates buying things like socks. She'd rather buy balloon-making kits or fish food that turns into live sea monkeys. It's a personality thing. She's totally impractical.

"Living in New Mexico would be different," my mother said. She took a bite of her Cocoa Krispies; then she folded her napkin into a pyramid and placed it next to her cereal bowl. "It wouldn't be just another apartment, another big city. New Mexico is a kind of door . . . it's a New World with Possibility."

"You got that line out of the atlas," I said, taking a bite of my dry toast. It was a caption underneath a picture of a giant cactus. The atlas had been lying open on the coffee table ever since her poetry phase ended, the phase in which she'd stood on the table for hours, reciting the poems of skinny old poets from my English lit book.

She shrugged. "Still, New Mexico would be better than here."

"I'm not kidding. I'm not going this time." I really meant it.

"We've been here too long, almost a year. If we moved to New Mexico, we could—"

I shoved the table and stood up, accidentally sloshing some milk out of her bowl. When I was young, moving around was okay; it was an adventure. But it's not fun anymore. I went outside and sat on the fire escape until she left for work.

When she came home that night, she tacked an O'Keeffe calendar page in the bathroom right across from the toilet. It was supposed to be a painting of a place called Palo Duro Canyon, but it looked more like a boiling red pit. It had swirling black lines and a spot of yellow burning in the middle. Except for one little patch of blue in the upper right corner, it fit my mood perfectly.

We avoided each other for at least twenty-four hours. I didn't look at her. She didn't look at me. On my calendar in my room, I drew a circle around the day spring break started. I was looking forward to it, especially because the LaGrones had invited me to go to the beach. We'd stay in a condo for nine whole days. Roo and I would have our own room with a television, refrigerator, bathroom, and everything.

"There's a long pier that stretches out into the water, where all the teenagers hang out at night," Roo had told me. "You're going to love it." I couldn't wait. I'd already made a list of what I needed to take. Everything was set.

Friday afternoon I started packing my suitcase. We'd leave on Saturday. I put in the usual things: shorts, T-shirts, underwear, pajamas. And I needed a flashlight. Roo said to bring one for when we walked on the beach at night.

I looked everywhere. The only place I hadn't checked was my mother's bedroom. We have an agreement. She doesn't get into my things. I don't get into hers. It's almost like a blood pact.

I knew I should wait until she got home from work, but I figured it wouldn't hurt to check just one place. There's three drawers on the top level of her dresser. I opened the one in the middle. In the front half were panties folded in neat square piles; no flashlight. I pushed my hand in farther, to the back of the drawer, and that's when I felt something hard.

It wasn't a flashlight. I could tell that. It was a box of some sort. The thought passed through my mind to just shut the drawer and go back to my room. But I didn't. I pulled it out into the light.

It was just an old Christmas card box, held together with a piece of string. It was dingy and worn, like something you'd find in an estate sale. Even the angel on the front had a World War II hairdo. It wasn't that interesting, and I knew it wasn't hiding a flashlight. Still, I untied the string.

Inside were several unused Christmas cards, each with the same angel holding a candle in one hand, an American flag in the other. But there was something else, underneath the cards.

I lifted them up and what I saw made me nearly stop breathing. It grabbed me in the pit of my stomach and wouldn't let go.

Underneath the cards were black-and-white photographs. That wasn't so strange. But one thing was weird—chilling. In the pictures my mother is standing in front of a Christmas tree with a man, or at least part of one. There was a hole in each picture, small and round, about the size of a dime, and it was right over his shoulders, exactly where his face should have been.

I shuffled through the photographs. Each one was the same. Someone—my mother, I was certain—

had taken manicure scissors or a razor and sliced all the way around the man's head. In each picture, one after the other, there was a ragged hole. I stood there, my heart thumping, trying to take in what it meant.

The photographs had been taken in an odd place, too, not in a living room where most people put Christmas trees. Behind the tree were shelves full of jars, things like home-canned tomatoes, jelly, and pickles.

I looked at the man again. Even without his head, he was big, taller than the tree and twice as big as my mother. Trembling, I held one of the photographs and looked closer. He wore cowboy boots with silver tips on the toes and starched blue jeans. Big hands hung loose at his sides like weights, and he wore a Western-style shirt with pearl buttons. And his belt buckle. It was big like rodeo cowboys wear, silver and shiny like the head of an ax.

None of my mother was missing. She was smiling like crazy, staring up at the hole where the man's face had been. I looked down at her hands. She held them together, curved under her stomach as if she were holding something. And she was, the most important detail of all. It was obvious. She was pregnant. From the looks of her, the photograph must have been taken just before I was born.

I was absolutely certain. There was only one person that man could be. I called Roo.

"What's up?" she asked.

I told her about the pictures. "Do you think your sister could drive you over?"

"Give me ten minutes."

I hung up the phone and lined up the photographs on the kitchen table. Ten holes in a row, all just alike. My mother must have planned to tuck them inside Christmas cards. Then she'd gotten mad about something and changed her mind. It was typical behavior for her. Only that time, she'd really done it. She'd messed up my whole life.

When Roo knocked on the door, I was pacing the floor. I led her into the kitchen.

"You really think that's your dad?" She picked up one of the photographs, wiggling her little finger through the hole.

"What do you think?" I answered. "It's obvious."

Roo shrugged. "I don't know. It could be your dad. But then again, it could be anybody. It's not like we can see his face."

"I know. That's the point. My mother wouldn't cut out just anyone's face. Plus I'm in the picture. Well, sort of."

I picked up one of the photographs and held it closer. Even though I couldn't see his head, the man seemed familiar. He was tall like me and large-boned. The hair on his arms looked blond, exactly like mine. He was definitely my father.

"If we had stayed in one place long enough, he would have found us," I said to Roo.

She grabbed me by the shoulders. "Shelby, listen. Your father does not live in a golden castle somewhere. Get real!" She picked up a magazine from the living room and flipped through the pages, holding the holes in the photographs to different faces. First she tried the faces in the male underwear ads. Then she tried a few movie stars.

"How about this one, Shelb?"

"Too young," I said, glancing up. The face staring through the hole looked about ten years old.

"Okay, here's an older one." Roo shoved the magazine at me.

The head of a toothless man grinned down at my mother. He was completely bald except for one strand of white hair that stuck up in front like the horn on a unicorn.

It was pretty funny, but my insides hurt and I felt like there was a hole cut out of me, too.

"Sorry," Roo said. "Didn't mean to upset you. Why don't you just ask your mom about it? Get it over with."

"I can't, not right before we leave on our trip. Plus I was snooping around. What would I be doing in her underwear drawer?"

"What *were* you doing there?" She grinned.

"I told you. Looking for the flashlight. She keeps things in weird places. Open our freezer. You'll find fourteen tubes of lipstick, a dozen bottles of nail polish, and a half-empty box of fish sticks."

Roo got up and opened the freezer door. "You forgot one thing: a . . . What *is* this, anyway?" She held up the frozen wishbone from a Thanksgiving turkey. Every place we moved to, my mother brought it.

"It's from the first turkey she ever cooked. I don't even remember it, but she thinks it's something to celebrate."

Roo laughed and shut the door.

"Anyway," I said, "even if I asked her about him, what makes you think she'd tell the truth? She obviously doesn't want me to know who my father is."

"You shouldn't jump to conclusions."

"This one's pretty logical," I answered. "We even look alike."

"Except for the face," she reminded me.

Before she left, she told me not to worry so much. "And forget the flashlight," she said. "We've got an extra one. You really need this trip to the beach. It'll do you good."

After I told her goodbye and shut the door, I put all the photographs back into the box inside my mother's drawer, except for one. I put that one into my journal, on the same page where Ishmael says it's "a damp, drizzly November in my soul."

Roo says it's morbid, keeping a journal of nothing but sad lines. I say, if you keep all the sad stuff in one place, there won't be as many surprises.

Later that night, before my mother got home, I opened my journal and looked at the photograph again. There was something about it that haunted me. It was like déjà vu, as if I'd been there somehow. But that didn't make any sense. I wasn't even born yet. The thought troubled me all night long.

Chapter Four

IT WAS LATE WHEN MY MOTHER GOT IN FROM work. I heard her open the refrigerator, as usual. I knew she'd eat two chocolate pudding snacks, watch the Home Shopping Network for a while, then go to bed. Usually, when I knew she'd gotten in okay, I'd go back to sleep. This night was different.

Every time I closed my eyes, I saw her and my headless father. Only the pictures weren't black and white anymore. They were red. And the shelves behind the Christmas tree weren't stacked full of jars of jelly and pickles, either. They were full of red clotted things, something that looked like heads bobbing in pickle brine.

The morning came slowly and I woke up tired.

I walked into the kitchen, where my mother sat at the table. With one hand she was dipping a tea bag in and out of a cup, as if she were in a trance. With the other she held a paper towel up to her nose. She was making soft sniffling noises, as if she'd been crying. One of her newspaper obituaries lay folded beside her.

"Hi," she said weakly.

I didn't answer. I'd planned to confront her with the pictures, but something was obviously wrong.

There wasn't a drop of coffee made. I searched around in the cabinet for the jar of instant.

"Have a good night's sleep?"

I still didn't answer.

"I've got hay fever," she said, sniffing. "We worked with ferns again last night, that's why. Did I wake you up when I came in?"

I shook my head, which was pounding from lack of sleep, from having nightmares all night long.

"Shelby?" She said my name like she does when she's about to lay something big on me.

"Last night I got a sign." When my mother says that, it means she's had a dream. She thinks they mean something.

I held my coffee cup under the faucet, filling it with water. Then, slowly, I sprinkled a spoon of freeze-dried coffee into it. The grains floated on the top like little black plastic boats, then sank, turning the water black. I shoved the cup into the microwave and sat down at the table right underneath one of Georgia O'Keeffe's cow skulls.

My mother was waiting. She'd cut a piece of toast into triangles and arranged it around a circle of scrambled eggs like a sun.

"For you!" she said, pushing the plate in front of me.

"Did somebody die?" I said finally, nodding toward the newspaper.

"Yeah, lots of them," she quipped. She picked up the paper and let it drop to the floor at her feet. "Like I told you, I'm allergic to those ferns. They make my nose run and my eyes swell up."

I picked up the pepper grinder. It's a battery-operated lighthouse. My mother got it for me years ago, right after we moved out of the women's shelter. We were only there for a month, and I don't exactly remember it, but she said we celebrated when we got our own place.

I pressed the button on the side. The light came on in the tower as it started grinding the peppercorns. It made a soft whir as I waved it over my eggs, sprinkling them with black.

My mother watched me for a minute; then she started up again. "Shelby, now listen. Last night I woke up and had a feeling someone was in the room. You know how it is sometimes? Anyway, I sat up. And you won't believe it! Guess who it was!"

I hate it when she does that. It could have been the Wicked Witch of the East. I didn't know or care.

"It was Georgia O'Keeffe! She was sitting in a chair next to my bed! I could have reached out and touched her!"

At this point, my mother jumped up from her chair and grabbed the string of garlic off the wall over our stove. It's a decoration, plus it's supposed to make us look like we're exotic cooks.

She took one end of the string in each hand and held it across her bathrobe like a lumpy smile. The whole time she was talking about dumb old Georgia and how she'd been holding a string of bones or something. Then it dawned on me.

"It sounds like that picture in your art book," I said. Georgia O'Keeffe, with her skinny black dress and pinched-up face, was holding the spinal column of some poor dead cow. It was just as my mother described. The old lady held one end of the string of bones in each hand, and it stretched across her dress like a big fat necklace.

My mother's dream wasn't a sign. It was a memory.

"After a few seconds," she continued, "one of the bones began to drop. It floated to the floor, real soft and quiet like snow, Shelby. Then the other bones floated down, one at a time. They hit the floor without even making a sound."

She bit her upper lip as if she didn't know whether to go on.

"The bedroom was perfectly quiet. Then, here comes the major part. She spoke to me! It was spooky! She said, 'Come pick up the bones, Zoe.' "

"After all that, that's all she had to say? Did you tell her you already had a turkey bone in the freezer?"

"I'm serious, Shelby. Anyway," she continued, "it was her voice that got to me. It sounded so far away, hundreds of miles away. But it was familiar. I sat there in bed trying to think whose it was. Then she spoke again: 'Come pick up the bones, Zoe.' That's when I knew."

She nibbled at a triangle of her toast. "It was as clear as day. Remember that elderly lady I lived with in Red Valley? The one who had a temporary foster home?"

I looked up.

"It was her voice, Aunt Onie's. I hadn't heard it in years."

"And you got up this morning and saw her obituary," I filled in. I knew she sometimes bought a newspaper from one of the larger towns near Red Valley.

"No, I didn't see her obituary. She's alive. I'm pretty sure."

I pressed the lighthouse button again, spraying pepper on my empty plate.

"That's the sign, Shelby."

"What?"

"Aunt Onie's voice. We have to go to Red Valley."

"Last week you dreamed you were at the mall shopping naked. You said you were being chased by a huge rooster. You didn't think we had to go visit a chicken farm."

"The problem is," my mother said slowly, "we can't wait until summer. We have to go now."

"I can't. I'm going to the beach, remember?"

"After this week I won't have any time off," my mother was saying. "On top of the regular funerals and weddings, we'll be pulling some all-nighters getting ready for the proms. If we're ever going to go, it's got to be now. Aunt Onie always wanted to see you."

"I thought the last time she saw you, you were a kid. I thought you hadn't talked to her since."

"Well, I did see her once. A long time ago, just before you were born."

"Just before?" I thought of the photographs, of my mother's big stomach.

"Oh, Shelby, I don't remember exactly when I was there. I've lost track of the time. Anyway, it's not important."

"It is to me."

She sighed real heavy. "I called the LaGrones."

"You did what?"

"They understood, Shelby."

"*They* understood!" My eyes stung. "What about *me*? Do you ever think about how I feel? Have you ever thought, one time in my life, how I feel about anything?"

"You can go to the beach with them anytime."

"I don't want to go *anytime*. I want to go now, this spring break. We have nine days all planned out." I stood up. "I can't believe you're doing this!"

She reached toward me, but I backed away. "Don't touch me!"

"Okay." She drew her hand back. "Shelby, please. Listen."

"No. I've heard enough."

I ran to the bathroom, slammed the door, and locked it. Georgia O'Keeffe's stupid canyon stared at me. I ripped it off the wall, threw it on the floor, and turned on the bathwater.

After a few minutes, when the water was so deep I knew it would run over the top when I got in, I saw my mother's note. It came sliding under the door on a piece of flowered stationery.

> *Dear Shelby,*
>
> *I'm sorry. I should not have called the LaGrones without telling you first.*
>
> *But we have to go to Red Valley. We have to. I promise we'll only stay a couple of days. Please, Shelby.*
>
> > *Love,*
> > *Mom*

I wadded up the note and stepped into the tub, scooting down so that the hot water slowly slid over my face.

I should have known something would happen to mess things up. With my mother, you can't count on anything.

I stayed in the tub a long time. By the time I got out, she'd left for work. Then Roo called.

"My mother told me the bad news."

"I hate her, Roo."

"No, you don't."

"Yes, I do. She's making me spend spring break with a hundred-year-old lady who lives in the middle of a cow pasture."

"She's that old?"

"Well, probably. She was old when my mother was a kid. She must be ancient now."

"I didn't know you had an aunt."

"I don't. She's not my aunt or anybody's. Anyway, my mother lied again. She always told me that she never went back to Red Valley, that it was too sad for her. Then she accidentally lets it out that she saw the old lady before I was born."

"So?"

"So why'd she lie?"

"Shelby, you're getting paranoid. Maybe she never told you because it wasn't important. People do see other people."

"I know. But this is different. I think it has something to do with my father. It's all connected."

"The only connections are the ones you're making in your own head. Keep to the facts, Shelby. It's called being rational."

"Right. You're the one who gets to lie out on the beach. It's easy for you to say not to worry."

"Look, you'll go with us this summer. You have to keep positive thoughts. Everything will be fine. Plus I'll bring you something. How about a baby starfish?"

"Okay, if it's already dried up. Just don't take it out of the sea."

"I won't," she said, and we told each other goodbye.

I spent the rest of the day by myself. I finished a book report on *Quo Vadis* that was due after the break and I watched a couple of movies. Late that afternoon I was lying on the floor in the living room watching *Ben-Hur* when my mother got home. She said a quick hello, then got her suitcase out of the hall closet and went straight to her room. In a few minutes she was back in the kitchen pulling her Georgia O'Keeffe calendar pages off the wall.

Pretty soon she came back into the living room, stood on the coffee table, and started pulling those calendar pages down. I punched up the volume on the remote. After a few minutes she stepped down and walked over to me, holding all her pictures.

"I'm ready to go, Shelby."

"What are you talking about?"

"To Red Valley."

"Now? I thought we were leaving in the morning. I'm right in the middle of the chariot race." I turned up the volume again so that the sounds of the horses pounded into the walls.

"We'll stop at a motel on the way," she shouted. "We'll find one of those places that gives you a free breakfast and has an indoor swimming pool. It'll be fun."

"Right," I murmured. I didn't move.

"I'm restless," she shouted.

"What else is new?" She didn't hear me, because she was already halfway down the hall.

Red Valley was at least ten hours away. We'd have to stop on the way, or it would be three or four in the morning before we got there.

After a few seconds she hollered at me from her room.

"Shelby, get your clothes."

There are times I can't talk any sense into her, and I could tell this was one of those. I got up slowly, turned off the television, and went to my room. My suitcase was already packed for the beach, but I grabbed an extra pair of jeans and an old T-shirt. I wasn't going to dress up for anyone in Red Valley.

At the last minute, I grabbed my journal of sad lines. In the middle was the saddest part of all, my mother and my headless father standing in front of a Christmas tree.

Chapter Five

WE'D BEEN ON THE ROAD FOR HOURS AND I'D had a lot of time to think. It wasn't because my mother had been quiet, though.

"Did I ever tell you about that bird we buried in the forest?"

She'd been talking forever.

"Shelby? Did I tell you about the bird?" she repeated, raising her voice.

I sighed, long and loud like an air mattress with the plug pulled out. When she was satisfied I was still awake, she continued.

"I found this dead bird out back in the forest at Aunt Onie's."

"I thought you said there weren't any trees in the Texas Panhandle." I'd caught her in another lie.

"Well, there are some. Aunt Onie planted a row of pine trees in her backyard. We called it a forest."

I leaned back and closed my eyes.

"Anyway, like I was trying to tell you, before

43

you kept making me lose my train of thought, I found this bird. Dead, of course."

"Of course."

"Shelby, stop interrupting me!"

"I'm not." I could lie too.

"In one way the bird we found was a common blackbird," she continued. "The wings were iridescent, you know, shiny, like the inside of an abalone shell."

"I know what *iridescent* means." I could have picked up fifty iridescent abalones at the beach.

"Well, that's what the wings looked like."

"I hate to tell you. The bird was a grackle," I mumbled. They flocked on the parking lot of our apartment building, looking for bits of garbage people dropped on their way to the Dumpsters.

My mother chattered on. "Aunt Onie said we should bury something valuable with the bird in case it was an Egyptian princess—you know, transformed, like Archy."

She was referring to Archy, the cockroach who had been a poet in a former life. During her poetry phase, she read the whole book aloud, how he had to jump on the typewriter keys to peck out a poem, and how his best friend was a cat named Mehitabel. The book was almost as dumb as Georgia O'Keeffe.

The drive kept getting longer and longer, and there hadn't been any decent motels, not a single one with an indoor pool or free breakfast.

"Shelby? Are you listening?"

I answered with another long sigh and my mother went on.

"Aunt Onie hunted around in her jewelry box and found a beautiful broken earring that looked exactly like a diamond, except it was blue."

I yawned. " 'All of Gaul is divided into three parts. . . .' " I quoted from my Latin assignment to see if she'd notice. She didn't.

"So we put the bird in this wooden tea box that had a sliding lid. Aunt Onie got it in San Francisco. Well, not her, a friend of hers. Anyway, we laid the bird in the box and we tucked the earring next to its wing. Then we buried it in the forest."

I opened my eyes. "You touched a dead bird? An egregious error." Ms. P. gave us extra credit if we recorded that we used a vocabulary word at least fifty times. I was too tired to get out my tablet, though. "I wouldn't touch a dead anything, especially a bird wearing an earring," I added.

She ignored me and went on to another story, something about a telescope. Aunt Onie had set it up on the back porch to try to see the rings of Saturn. I closed my eyes again. Maybe I could go to sleep and wake up and this would all be a bad dream: finding the photographs, the trip to Red Valley, everything.

It would be night and I'd be sitting on the dock with Roo watching for tarpon. She says you can see them sometimes if the moonlight's right. They slap the top of the water and roll on their sides. That's when you see the silver, like sparks coming up out of the water. She says they glitter like minnows, only they're giant, about six feet long. They have silver scales that can get as big as the palm of your hand.

Here, there was nothing but black road. The miles clicked on and on as we got farther and farther away from home.

I stared out into the light from our headlights. I saw my father's shiny belt buckle, his big hands, and the hole where his head should have been. I shook my head and the vision ended.

There was absolutely nothing ahead of us. The night was a giant mouth waiting for us to drive inside. The stars were teeth. They weren't in neat rows, either, where you could dodge them. They clamped down on you in every direction.

It was about three in the morning when we finally got outside Red Valley. I looked out expecting to see the lights of the town, but only three or four blinked in the distance, and those seemed as if they could go out any minute because of the wind. It's the wind my mother said she remembered most about Red Valley. She said that once when she opened a car door, the wind whipped around and yanked it off by its hinges.

Our car began to rock. It slid back and forth across the yellow stripe on the highway. We drove on, but my mother gripped the steering wheel and leaned forward, willing the car to stay on the road.

Suddenly she'd had enough. She pulled off the road. "We better stop here," she said. "I'm afraid we're going to get blown over."

I looked out. The headlights were still on and I could see that we were in an abandoned gas station. It was a small flat-roofed building made of big brown stones cemented together. The door had a screen ripped to shreds and the door itself hung halfway open as if no one had even bothered to lock it. Two rusty pumps leaned in clumps of broken concrete. It looked like something from an old *Twilight Zone* episode.

My mother stopped in the cracked drive and turned off the ignition. "Get some sleep, Shelby. When the sun comes up, we'll find our way around."

"You've got to be kidding!" I sat straight up. "Serial killers hang out in places like this!"

She rolled her sweater into a lump for a pillow, propped it against the window, and went right to sleep.

Me, I sat in the dark and listened to the wind. It had picked up even more, making strange swishing sounds all around us, a giant broom trying to sweep us off the earth. Something, a broken bottle or a can, kept rolling back and forth, scraping across the broken pavement, and the screen door of the station squeaked on its hinges, blowing open and shut, over and over.

There was no way I could sleep. Every time I closed my eyes, I felt myself sinking into the black hole on top of my father's shoulders. I twirled around and around in space as if I were falling through a deep tunnel down into a well. And when I hit the bottom, I found myself in Aunt Onie's forest. Except there weren't any trees. There was a row of scarecrows dancing in the wind. They all had missing heads.

Chapter Six

THE SUN POUNDED ON MY FACE THROUGH the windshield.

I groaned and tried to stretch; then I remembered where we were. I needed a bathroom and a cup of coffee.

"Can you make it five more minutes?" My mother started the car.

"What if I say no?" I grumbled.

We pulled out of the drive and back onto the highway.

"Look, Shelby. Outside."

"What?" I didn't see anything except dirt blowing across the road.

"The horizon. I didn't even notice it when I lived here. You can see all the way to the edge, where the sky touches down. There's not one thing to block your view."

"I like things to block my view," I said. "Trees and mountains. Sunbathers on the beach."

"Did I tell you that Georgia O'Keeffe lived around here at one time? It was the turning point, the one I told you about, before she moved to New Mexico."

I looked out the window. She must have lived in a prettier place than this. Red Valley was brown and shriveled like a mole on an old lady's neck. Nothing about it was red. And nothing about it was a valley. It was the last place in the world I'd choose to live.

We drove down Main Street, which consisted of a single row of one-story buildings. They were brown, too, only they were thin and flat like dried-up bread crusts. One streetlight swung on a wire stretched across the road. If it went out, the whole town would be dead.

"I bet there's not a mall within two hundred miles," I remarked. If there were one, it'd be crowded with people wearing spidery hair nets and using walkers to get around. Nobody in this town would be under eighty.

"There's the bus station." My mother pointed at a drugstore on the corner named Henry's. New Year's Eve decorations still hung in the window.

"That's where I got off the bus the night I came back."

"A little girl got off the bus? At night?"

"I mean, another time I came here. I was grown."

"Why did you? Come back, I mean."

She pulled over to the side of the road across from the drugstore. "Come on, you're making a big thing out of nothing." She was about to get irritated, but she softened her voice.

"Let's go in. We'll get some breakfast, and I'd like to pick out some kind of little gift for Aunt Onie."

"They probably have plenty of crocheted toilet-paper holders and laxatives," I said.

She ignored me and got out of the car, then waited for me.

"It smells like an enema bag in here," I whispered as we walked inside.

"Shhh." My mother nodded toward the back of the store. I looked up and saw a row of four cowboy hats. The men had their backs to us and were talking low and drinking coffee at the soda fountain counter.

I didn't care if they heard me or not. I picked up a boot-shaped toothpick holder that had WELCOME TO TEXAS stamped on the front and pretended to be looking at it. "You could get her this," I said. "If she's still got any teeth to pick."

"Can I help y'all?" A shrill voice echoed from behind the fountain counter. I looked up just in time to see the cowboy hats turn toward us.

There were a couple of real old men, then one about middle age. The last one sat with his back to us, but his shoulders looked young.

"Y'all like a cup of coffee?" The woman behind the counter grinned at us. The first thing I noticed was her hair. It was pale pink and whipped on top of her head like a Dairy Queen ice-cream cone. Two long curls hung past her ears like fishhooks.

"My daughter would probably like a rest room," my mother called out. I thought I'd die.

"Go on, Shelby." She pushed me. "I'll just look around a minute."

The woman at the counter hollered toward the end of the counter. "Reese, go back there and move those boxes so the little lady can find her way to the john."

The cowboy on the end turned and slid off the stool. He was probably a little older than me. He had a toothpick in the corner of his mouth and he wore boots, jeans, and a cowboy shirt. His belt buckle was silver and was the size of a butter dish. I didn't need his help.

I walked ahead of him toward the back of the store, where signs tacked on the wall said POST OFFICE and BUS SCHEDULE. Another sign pointed to the rest room.

"This is really the bus station?" I asked.

"Buses come through here. Sometimes one or two people get off, a couple get on. It's not exactly a regular bus station. From Dallas to Amarillo you're going to stop about nine times. This is just one of those stops."

I could see leaving a town like Red Valley. I couldn't see getting off the bus to stay.

"Where y'all headed?" he asked.

"Here, I guess." I looked at my feet. "We're coming to see some old lady friend of my mother's." I reached over and kicked one of the boxes out of the way. "I can get in the door by myself."

"What's her name?" he asked, leaning against the wall while I moved the boxes. "The lady y'all are coming to see."

"Aunt Onie Somebody," I said as I shut the door harder than I needed to.

"Purdy," he shouted through the door. "Onie Purdy. The Angel Lady."

"The what?" I asked when I came out. He was still leaning against the wall, chewing on his toothpick, one thumb hooked under his giant belt buckle. He'd probably heard me use the bathroom and everything.

"The Angel Lady." He grinned from the side of his mouth opposite the toothpick. "She claims angels live on her roof. Says they signal lost children where to come. Y'all wouldn't be lost, by any chance?" He grinned again, then pulled his toothpick out of his mouth and broke it in half.

"No, we're not lost. We're here for a couple of nights, then we're heading back home." To civilization, I thought.

Angels lived on her roof. We were on our way to spend the night in the house of some kind of psycho, an old one.

The cowboy took his hat off and rubbed his forehead where there was a dent from wearing the thing so much. He probably even slept in it.

"I didn't think she had any kin," he said.

"We're not related," I said, emphasizing the *not*. "My mother stayed with her one time. It was before I was born."

"One of the foster kids?"

I shrugged. He was starting to get on my nerves.

I looked around the store. I hoped my mother had found some kind of gift so we could go and get our visit over with. Maybe I could even talk her into leaving before we spent the night.

I told the cowboy I had to leave; we were in kind of a hurry. But when I got back to the soda fountain, my mother was sitting on a stool sipping a cup of tea like she had all the time in the world.

"Sit down, Shelby," she said as I approached the counter. "I ordered you some pancakes, or flapjacks, as the menu says. Now, where's that ladies' room?"

Before I had a chance to say anything, she left me there.

The woman behind the counter adjusted the dish towel she had tied around her waist. She said goodbye to the cowboys, who were leaving too. The young one, Reese, tipped his hat and said, "See ya later."

Right, I thought, when I join the rodeo circuit.

"So. Your mama told me your name's Shelby," said Pink Hair. "She said you were named after some kind of meadow or something. See, I'm real interested in what things mean, especially names. Want some cocoa?"

"Coffee," I said, "black."

"Bad for your kidneys. Anyway, as I was telling your mama, my name's Teena. That's Teena with two *e*'s, not an *i*."

About a dozen pearls dangled from miniature gold chains at her ears. Her fingernails, which matched her lips, were bright red and looked like press-ons. She was John D.'s perfect woman.

"Your mama's got an odd name, too, nearly as odd as yours. She said Zoe means something like Eve, you know, from the Garden of Eden. My name, like I said, is Teena. It's religious. Well, it is if you're starting with Christina. Christina, of course, isn't my name, but it's the closest thing, on account of you can't find Teena in any name book."

She set a cup of coffee in front of me and said my flapjacks would be ready in a jiff.

"Zoe says y'all plan to be here for a few days—"

I interrupted. "Not a few. A couple."

"Anyway," she continued, "I invited y'all to the street festival tonight. I'm Red Valley's Sorghum Queen." She stood back, waiting for me to get the full effect.

I turned around to see if my mother was coming from the rest room. She'd stopped at one of the aisles to look at something. When she saw me, she held a box in the air. "What about a jigsaw puzzle, Shelby? This one's got a deer on it. She'd like that."

Teena hollered back, "Miss Purdy can't see that good anymore." She turned to me and said, "The poor thing don't ever even come out of her house hardly, except to sit outside and carve. One of these days she's gonna cut her hand off and nobody'll know until she bleeds to death and it's too late."

"Does she have any relatives or anything around?"

"Nobody who ever stays."

I understood that perfectly. We hadn't been here a half hour and I was ready to leave.

"Sometimes I take her Dr Peppers over to her. She has to have a case and they have to be those little-bitty glass bottles. She won't drink nothing out of a can. And she don't like how the big bottles feel in her hand."

She held a fork alongside my head next to my right ear.

"Can you see the fork?"

"I guess," I mumbled, feeling kind of nervous. "Do you think my pancakes are done?"

She ignored me. "Now, Miss Purdy wouldn't be able to see that fork. She can't see that good to the side. Here, try this." She picked up the saucer from under my coffee cup and held it in front of my face.

"Now, pretend you got a blind spot in front of you. That's how it is for her. It's like she can't see good in the center or the sides. It's some kind of Retin-A Congeneration is how it was explained to me."

Retinal degeneration. I learned about it in Health Occupations. So now we were going to spend the night with a psycho old blind person.

The sooner we got back home, the better.

"Your mama likes to wear black, don't she? She's not in any kind of motorcycle gang, is she?" My mother was wearing one of her Georgia O'Keeffe outfits. She had on black jeans, a black turtleneck, and black boots. Of course, O'Keefe never dressed exactly like that, but it was my mother's version.

"My mother's never even been on a motorcycle, that I know of. She just likes to wear black. No reason." I wasn't about to get into her artist obsession.

Teena stood with her hands on her hips. "Me, I like red. I had my colors done and I'm a Summer, which means I'm not supposed to wear just any shade of red, though. I can wear the powder-blues, lemon-yellows, colors like that. Hey, if y'all stay, I could do your colors. You have to tie a white towel around your neck and look at your skin color."

She studied my face. "You're probably a Spring, based on the strawberry-blond hair. Betcha look real good in avocado, don't you?"

I shrugged. I didn't know what I looked good in. It wouldn't be anything called avocado.

Finally Teena shoved a plate of pancakes in front of me.

"Did I hear you say Aunt Onie is losing her vision?" my mother asked when she sat down.

"Like I was telling Shelby here . . ." Teena started up again, holding the fork alongside my mother's ear. I tuned her out as I poured syrup on my pancakes. Too bad Roo couldn't be here. She'd be laughing her head off.

I looked at my watch. We'd been here forty-five minutes.

"You divorced or what?" Teena was saying to my mother, not even giving her time to answer.

"Me, I'm presently single. My last boyfriend, we had matching shirts and everything, but it didn't work out. He came over to my house one day wearing this cap with a flashlight taped on top. He'd used a gob of Scotch tape, let me tell you. Anyway, he claimed he wanted to inspect my foundation." She put her hands on her hips and raised her eyebrows. Then she began to replay the whole thing.

" 'You want to inspect *my what*?' I said."

" 'I just want to check and make sure you don't have termites,' he said."

While she talked I watched her false eyelashes. They were the longest I'd ever seen. When she got to talking real fast, they hit the bottoms of her eyebrows like a shutter flapping up.

"When he said that about termites, I said, 'No sir.' I wasn't letting just anybody check out my foundation. I decided that was just too odd. Things shouldn't be too odd, you know. Besides, I have a child and you can't be too careful. Is Shelby your only one?"

My mother said yes, stirring her spoon around in her cup.

"I got me a little boy. He's four. Twenty-two hours in labor with that kid. Nine and a half pounds, twenty-one inches long. I had to have sixteen stitches and—" Before she had a chance to launch into any more details, my mother stopped her.

"How's Aunt Onie doing, besides not being able to see too well?"

"Her heart's bad," Teena said. "She's just hanging on by a thread. You can't really tell it, though. She's spunky."

Blind psycho old person, hanging on by a thread. I couldn't wait.

We finished our breakfast and my mother looked around a bit more. Finally she found a gift for Aunt Onie. It was a ceramic blackbird with its mouth wide open.

"It's a spoon holder for your stove," Teena explained. "I've got one just like it. Except mine's a pig." She demonstrated how you put the spoon in its mouth.

"Can we go now?" I asked. I wasn't looking forward to Aunt Onie, but I'd had enough of Teena.

"Would y'all mind taking Miss Purdy's Dr Peppers, since y'all are going out there anyhow?" Teena asked.

My mother said we wouldn't and we finally headed out to the car, me walking behind with the case of drinks.

We'd used up at least an hour. In fact, my mother had been stalling ever since we got to Red Valley. We could have already been out to Aunt Onie's and gotten our visit halfway over.

I wasn't too happy to find out that Aunt Onie was nearly blind and partly crazy. I'd hoped maybe I could show her the photograph in my journal, that maybe she'd know something about my father, but now it was beginning to sound as if that wouldn't be possible.

We finally got in the car and drove down Main Street away from the center of town. It was already midmorning. I was tired and my mother was too.

"How much longer will it take to get to her house?"

"Not too long. She lives past town, though."

Pretty soon the paved roads turned to dirt and there were fewer and fewer houses. The sky wasn't blue anymore. It had filled with heavy-looking clouds. As we headed out to Aunt Onie's house, the day hung before us gray and uncertain.

Chapter Seven

IN THE COUNTRY, THE LAND STRETCHED ALL around in smooth long sheets. My mother loved it. "When you run through tall grass, it's like water. You look back, and your footprints are gone. You can actually get lost."

I doubted that. There were plenty of markers, rusted cars and plows, probably even cow skulls. Nothing disappeared out here.

"Georgia O'Keeffe even got lost one time. I read about it."

"That's nice," I answered. My mother hates it when I say that.

"She had to wait until night. When the North Star came out, she knew which way to go. That's when she started her evening star pictures. She kept painting different versions, trying to paint exactly how she felt."

"She should have bought a compass." If anybody got on my nerves, it was Georgia O'Keeffe. I could just see the skinny old lady lost and running in circles in the field. No wonder so many of her paintings had doors and windows. She was always trying to find her way in or out of something.

My mother gazed out the window.

" 'Our sweetest songs are those that tell of saddest thought,' " she recited. It was a line from one of the poems she'd studied during her poetry phase. I'd heard it lots of times.

"There's a little country cemetery a couple of miles from here." She slowed the car to a stop and pointed down a crooked road.

"When I was a little girl, I went out there with Aunt Onie. She wanted to see her parents. Well, not actually see them, you know." She laughed nervously. We sat there as if she couldn't decide what to do, turn down the cemetery road or go straight.

"You're not planning on driving out there, are you?" I looked at my watch. "You already know she's not dead." Aunt Onie was probably half dead, but according to Teena, she still chewed tobacco and drank at least two Dr Peppers every day.

My mother has always liked side trips. Once on the way to visit a lighthouse at Port Isabel, she took a turn and we wound up at a broken-down trailer house with a sign out front that said SNAKE LADY.

A huge lady with a real snake hanging around her neck came out onto the porch. She was wearing a red satin robe, had about six rings on each finger, and was waving around a plastic shovel in one hand. She hollered at us, offering to sell us a glow-in-the-dark pooperscooper. My mother actually started to get out of the car, but I stopped her. We don't even have any pets. It seems like I'm the only one with sense in our family.

"We're both tired," I said, wondering how much farther it was to Aunt Onie's. "Let's just hurry up and get there."

My mother agreed, starting down the straight road again. It was unpaved and narrow, lying before us like a thin brown strip shaved out of the fields. By now she was sitting straight up, tense. Her knuckles were white on the steering wheel.

Something in Red Valley bothered her. For me, the place was too quiet, almost as if we were actually in a cemetery, only without neatly trimmed grass and flowers. Here, the tombstones were rusted-out cars and empty houses that stuck to the ground like sores, the grassy fields growing up all around them.

We drove on, passing an old school bus halfway buried in the ground, its front end sticking up like the carcass of a yellow beast. On television, they have those air freshener commercials that make you think the country is a place you want to bottle up and take home. They hadn't been out here. It was spooky.

Roo would be on the beach by now, hunting for treasures washed up by the ocean. In her bedroom she has a huge glass bottle filled with bits of driftwood, shells, and sea stones.

My mother rolled down the window and let the wind whip her hair. The smell of dryness and dirt blew into the car. You wouldn't find anything pretty to put into a jar out here. I decided it was time to ask.

"When you came here on the bus, you were pregnant with me, right? It must have been around Christmas, right?" I know because I was born soon after.

I'd caught her unprepared and she stiffened up against the steering wheel. "Not now, Shelby," she said.

Roo's got her birth on a videotape. Her father's grinning into the camera like crazy. My mother has never even wanted to talk about my birth, much less show pictures of it. In her opinion, I was born. That's it.

"When you were pregnant with me, did you come to see anyone else, besides Aunt Onie?"

"Shelby. No. Anyway, that's enough. It's hard for me, coming here."

"But why? Why is it hard?" I pushed.

My mother sighed, refusing to answer. We turned onto a caliche road, which is not quite paved but a little bit better than packed-down dirt. A gray-haired man in overalls and a dirty white T-shirt was burning trash in a barrel off the side of the road. He stirred the fire with a stick and the wind blew bits of charred paper around his face. He waved as we drove by.

"If it's so hard for you to come back here to Red Valley, then why did we?"

My mother slowed down to let some chickens run in front of the car.

"I asked you a question."

"I guess it's . . . closure, like reading the last chapter in a book. And the dream, of course, Aunt Onie's calling me. Look, we're almost there."

"What happened in Red Valley? I know something did." I pushed at the edges, trying to feel whether I'd gone too far yet.

"I was too young to be having a baby, I know that." She pressed her lips together like she'd come to the end of a seam and tied the knot hard.

I know when my mother is through answering questions. You might as well quit trying. She completely changed the subject.

"Maybe we'll drive to Canyon, see the college where Georgia O'Keeffe taught. I heard she wanted to paint her room black, but they wouldn't let her."

"Smart move." Then I added, "I have a favor to ask. I want you to promise not to say anything else about Georgia O'Keeffe. I'm sick of her." It was a way to get back at her for not answering any of my questions. I knew she'd agree. She wanted me in a good mood when we finally got to Aunt Onie's.

The house was pushed back off the road in a bare spot of land. Fifty years ago the wood on the outside probably looked decent. It was probably painted. Two fake deer with paint peeling off their backs and a miniature windmill decorated the yard, if you wanted to call it a yard. It was mostly hard-packed dirt and weeds.

Behind the house was an outhouse and a broken-down barn that looked like it had been stepped on. Beyond that was a windmill. Two of the blades were broken, but it still turned. Closer to the house, in the back, was a thin scrawny row of about six pine trees. You could even see bagworms in the branches.

The trees stood at the edge of the yard, all skimpy and embarrassed-looking.

"That's the forest?" I couldn't believe anyone would even refer to such a thing as a forest.

"It was bigger when I was a child," my mother said. "It towered over me like the dark forest in 'Hansel and Gretel.' We used to pretend Aunt Onie was the witch, only she was good. She didn't bake children in her oven."

As we came up closer toward the front of the house, we saw Aunt Onie. It was almost as if she were waiting for us. She sat in a straight-back chair on the porch, a porch that wrapped all the way around the house. Behind her in the picture window was a plastic Santa Claus face with red lit-up cheeks.

"What's with the Santa Claus?" We slowed to a stop in the dirt road in front of the house.

"She likes Christmas," my mother said, pulling the keys out of the ignition.

"It passed three months ago."

"Not for her." We sat in the car for a few moments. The old woman never even looked up. She was busy carving a piece of wood.

"Is she deaf or something?" I asked. She didn't act like she heard us at all. I was about to add it to the list: *blind, psycho, old, hanging on by a thread,* and *deaf.*

"She's concentrating on the wood. She used to say something was trapped inside it. She had to keep carving until it came out."

"Crazy," I murmured.

"She's real serious about her wood carving. Every child that came to stay here got something special carved just for him, or for her. It was birds mostly. Doves, quail, mockingbirds, all different kinds. Aunt Onie tried to capture the spirit of each child." My mother rested her forearms on the base of the steering wheel and watched out the window.

"What did she carve for you?"

"A wren, I think. I left it somewhere." She looked down at her hands. "It's the only thing I ever lost that I wish I still had."

"Are we getting out or not?" The sooner we got this trip over with the better.

"Everything's kind of rushing at me all at once." She put her face in her hands. "Maybe we shouldn't have come."

"Fine with me," I grumbled. "Let's go home."

My mother finally opened the car door. Reluctantly, I followed. We headed up toward the porch.

Aunt Onie was ancient, just as I'd expected. She looked like one of those dolls people make out of dried-up apples, like she'd baked in the sun for about a hundred years.

"Aunt Onie?" my mother called. She walked up closer and unhooked the wire latch on the gate. I stayed behind.

Aunt Onie looked up. "Zoe? Is that you, honey?" She brushed the wood shavings off her apron and stood. She was tall and thin and brown from being out in the sun and wind.

"Zoe?" she said again.

"Yes, ma'am. It's me." My mother had become a child again.

Aunt Onie grinned real wide and set her knife and wood on the chair.

"I was hoping you'd come." Her voice was thin and watery, and when she walked toward us, she came slow like something in a dream, her dress hanging down almost to the toes of her shoes.

Her shoes surprised me. They were sneakers, white with purple stripes on the sides.

"Come on up, Shelby," my mother directed. She looked back at me. I knew that once I got past the gate I'd be stuck.

I got hugged first. Aunt Onie wrapped her thin arms around me and held on forever. She felt like bones wrapped in Jell-O, hard and squishy at the same time, and she smelled like the inside of an old paper sack.

She kept on squeezing. I wondered if she was going to stand there hanging on to me until she died of a heart attack or a stroke. Somebody would have to peel her off of me. She kept saying my name over and over. It made me nervous.

Finally, she let go and went to my mother. Her hug lasted twice as long.

"I knew you'd come," Aunt Onie said to my mother, stepping back. She gazed at me. "Shelby don't take after you much, does she? She's a lot sturdier."

I shifted my weight, feeling even more un-comfortable.

Aunt Onie reached inside the front buttons of her dress, pulled out a handkerchief, and dabbed at her eyes. They looked too clear and blue to be nearly blind.

"Are you making another bird?" my mother asked.

"Might be, honey. Don't know yet." Aunt Onie picked up the piece of wood and ran her fingers over the knotty parts.

"Mostly it still is birds, seems like. Takes me a good bit longer than it used to, though. With this old mesquite I pick up around here, I have to keep sharpening my knife. Mesquite wood's a whole lot harder than oak. Four times, they say."

It looked as if she'd already sharpened the knife too many times. Her hands, which were as knotty as the wood, were full of cuts, some painted with stripes of red Merthiolate, others wrinkled into hard white scars.

She must have seen me looking at her hands, because she pointed to one of the red stripes. "Monkey Blood," she said. "They don't make medicine like that today. It sure heals 'em up."

Then she held up the piece of wood she'd been carving. "This one's for Shelby," she said proudly.

"How'd you know I'd be here?"

"The birds told me." She grinned and picked up her knife. She turned it toward the wood, shaving a wide curl that flew to the ground next to my foot.

"Aunt Onie, I'm so glad to see you," my mother said, hugging her again. "It's been too long."

"You're back. That's all that counts," the old lady said. "Seems to me yestiddy you was here. Now you're here again. Ain't no time passed, honey, 'cause I'm so glad to see you."

"I'm sorry that we never could come before. I think you know . . . you know . . . we've moved a lot of times."

My mother owed her more of an apology than that. If we could move around all over the country, we could have come here sooner. Aunt Onie, though, was a whole lot more forgiving.

"You're here now. That's enough, honey."

"I like those fancy running shoes," my mother said.

Aunt Onie lifted her skirt so that we could see them better. "Look at the back of them!" She turned and walked away from us so that we could see the red lights flashing on the heels.

"You girls, come on in this house," she said, opening the door.

It was dark. The curtains were drawn and the wood floor was worn and scuffed in the parts you could see. The rest was covered with small rugs, little circles that stuck to the wood like upside-down clouds. It looked like O'Keeffe's cloud painting, only the floor wasn't blue.

To the far right, in the corner, was a full-size bed and a small dresser with a mirror. There was a curtain on a rod that could be pulled around the bed, like what you might see in a hospital.

"You still sleep out here by the door, Aunt Onie? Just in case?"

"Still do," she answered. "Just in case anyone comes in the night. The county thinks I'm too old to keep kids. Still, if one got lost . . ." She stopped in mid-sentence and wandered into the kitchen. My mother and I walked on into the living room.

"Nothing's changed much," my mother said. She turned slowly, looking at everything. "I always loved this old house. There are so many places to hide."

A lit-up row of Christmas lights had been strung across the mantel. Along with the Santa face I'd seen from outside, they gave the room a reddish glow. There wasn't a television or a telephone.

"Guess which one's me," my mother said, pointing to a row of photographs tacked to the wall with straight pins.

I went right to the picture. My mother was just a little girl, sitting inside a small opening under the porch steps. She held a kitten in her lap.

The other photographs were children, too, all kids who had stayed with Aunt Onie before they went on to someplace else.

After I'd looked at all the pictures, I excused myself.

You'd think a big house would have more than one rest room, but it didn't. There wasn't even a shower. I turned on the water at the sink to wash my hands. It made a loud noise like a foghorn, and the water came out in brown spurts. One small chunk of brownish soap sat in a pink soap dish. I opened the medicine cabinet above the sink to see if there was a fresh bar. There wasn't; only three bottles of Merthiolate and a box of Band-Aids sat on the glass shelf.

I let the water run until it turned clear, then washed my hands without soap and dried them on the stiff pink towel hanging by the sink. I walked back into the living room.

Aunt Onie was sitting in the rocking chair, pushing at the floor with the toes of her shoes. My mother was curled up on the couch, her head on a crocheted pillow. She was sound asleep.

I sat down in a big chair with lace doilies covering the back and arms.

"So you're the baby," Aunt Onie said. "I never got to see the baby."

"I'm fourteen," I reminded her.

"When you get to my age, fourteen years is a minute. Your mama's been gone from Red Valley about a minute." She grinned, and when she did, her whole face wrinkled into lines.

I cleared my throat. I was thinking about how to say the words. I could come right out and ask. Do you know who my father is? Or I could ask about when I was a baby, why she'd never gotten to see me, why my mother had left and had never returned. I cleared my throat again, looking at my mother. She was snoring a little.

A chill spread across my body. I wrapped my arms around myself and looked at her, then at Aunt Onie. I felt scared of what I wanted to ask.

Aunt Onie rocked back and forth slowly, watching me.

"You want me to rock you?"

"Huh?" I shook my head. Roo would never believe this, not in a million years. A hundred-year-old lady asking if I wanted to sit in her lap. I felt my face redden.

"When your mama first come here, when she was a little bitty thing, I had to let the dishes go, laundry, everything." She paused. "I didn't do nothing but rock her, day and night, night and day." She rocked gently, pushing at the floor with her toes.

"She was so empty, you know."

"Her parents couldn't take care of her."

"Um-hm." She rocked back and forth, remembering. I couldn't imagine children in Aunt Onie's lap. She must've been soft, then.

"Her daddy lifted his hand one too many times."

"He hit her?" My mother had told me her parents couldn't keep her. Somehow I'd never thought to ask why.

"Yes, honey."

"Her mother died." I knew that much. She hadn't told me about the other.

"Um-hm. After that, that's when she come here and needed to be rocked so much. Course, I rocked her when she was growed up, too." My heart pounded.

"She came in on the bus, didn't she?" I whispered.

"Yes, she did. It was past midnight, about two A.M. Sheriff found her lying on the bench outside Henry's. She said she was waitin' for morning, but he brought her on out. It was snowing, and all she had on was a sweater. You could barely see the road by the time she got here."

"I wasn't with her."

"Not quite. You come along right after that."

"Why did she come here? And where had she been?"

Aunt Onie rocked back and forth, scraping her toes at the floor.

"Your mama never told you?"

"Uh-uh." I shook my head. My mouth had turned dry and my hands had turned cold. It was my father I wanted to know about.

Aunt Onie stopped rocking. She sat there perfectly still like a cemetery statue. I didn't think she'd ever start talking again.

"Go on," I urged. "She's a heavy sleeper." My mother was totally out.

Aunt Onie folded her hands in her lap; then she began again. "Your mama moved away. Wanted to live in the city by herself." She rocked back and forth, slowly, thinking and watching me.

"She came back, I 'spect, because she was about to have a baby. Girls want their mamas, you know. I was the closest thing." She stopped, pressing her lips together in a thin line.

She'd left out the part I really wanted to know about. I was about to just come out and ask her about him, but I didn't get a chance because she suddenly rocked forward in her chair and started singing.

" 'One little bird without any home, one tree that stands all alone—come build your nest in the branches tall, I'll rock you to and fro.' "

It was the song my mother sang to me when I was little, practically every night before I went to sleep.

My mother sat up, rubbing her eyes. I'd have to wait for any more answers.

Later, Aunt Onie showed me to my room in the attic. It was small, with two long skinny beds, each about as wide as a cot. I picked the one next to the wall because it had a small square window above it. I'd be able to see outside onto the roof where the angels hung out. They were probably up there now, twirling around in the wind like broken weather vanes.

I took my journal out of my suitcase, pulled down the bedspread, and stretched out. The sheets smelled like a basement. I rolled up the pillow, which was thin and lumpy. It felt like it'd been stuffed with oatmeal. Finally, I lay there, staring up at the water stains, thin rusty circles on the ceiling, mirroring the circle rugs Aunt Onie had plastered all over the floors.

I opened my journal and read a few lines from T. S. Eliot. "I have heard the mermaids singing, each to each. / I do not think that they will sing to me. . . ." Roo thinks that part is dumb. How can you hear mermaids and not have them singing to you?

I turned a couple of pages to part of a William Blake poem: "The night was dark, no father was there. . . ." I flipped past a few more pages to the photograph. A thin blue line of the journal page crossed my father's missing face where his smile should have been. I picked up the photograph, examining it again, trying to find the one clue I'd missed.

I turned the picture around and around, looking at it from every angle. There was nothing except a vague uneasy feeling brewing deep down inside of me like a storm warning.

Roo says you should fight anxiety with humor. I poked my finger through the hole in the photo and drew a smiley face on the end of it with a ballpoint pen. She would approve.

Finally, I laid the photograph back into the journal, on top of the page with Blake's line, and shut the book.

Before I fell asleep, I thought about what my mother had said about the hiding places in Aunt Onie's house. In one of those, I hoped to find the secret of my father.

Chapter Eight

WHEN I WOKE UP, THE ROOM WAS FULL OF shadows. I must have slept past lunch. I walked down the narrow stairs toward the kitchen, where my mother was drinking a cup of hot tea. The table was covered in a yellow plastic cloth with little red teapots printed on it. Friendly red spurts of steam rose merrily from the teapots like musical notes. Aunt Onie was standing at the stove stirring something with a large wooden spoon. The kitchen smelled like a holiday. It was warm and sweet, cheerful, like a page out of a first-grade reading book.

"Sleep well?" my mother asked.

"I should've brought my own pillow," I said, rubbing my neck.

"Sorry. Anyway, Aunt Onie and I were talking. We thought we'd go downtown to the street festival. Teena will be performing, and there'll be some crafts and food. We'll go for about an hour or so."

The food part sounded okay, but the rest sounded totally boring. I'd rather watch two episodes of *Mister*

Rogers than have to look at crafts. I knew what it would be like, long tables displaying picture frames made out of Popsicle sticks and refrigerator magnets made out of can lids.

"There's nothing else for you to do," she reminded me when I started to object.

She was right about that. In the rush to leave, I'd forgotten my headphones. I hadn't even brought a book. Aunt Onie had a few, but nothing I wanted to read. She lived in the Dark Ages. She was practically Amish.

"I thought you said they had food at the festival," I whispered. Aunt Onie was obviously cooking something.

"It's called hospitality, Shelby," my mother whispered back. She gave me a look that meant *You will eat something*.

When I saw the thick noodles and broth Aunt Onie dipped into our bowls, I remembered how long it had been since I'd eaten. We'd had pancakes in the morning and skipped lunch.

Along with the soup, Aunt Onie placed a bowl of stewed tomatoes on the table and several jars of homemade pickles.

"My pickles are almost gone," she remarked. "Don't have any left in the cellar. I have a couple of jars of green beans and tomatoes up here in the house. I don't do much canning anymore."

My mother said she remembered the big canning pot boiling on the stove, Aunt Onie pouring the hot liquid into the jars, placing the tops just so, screwing on the rings, and finally checking after they'd cooled to see that they'd sealed properly. She said that if they didn't seal, you could get botulism in just one bite.

I looked at the bowl of tomatoes and wondered if they'd been sealed.

My mother was looking at them too. "These tomatoes are out of your garden, aren't they?" she asked.

"Lordy, yes. They was canned some time ago. I had to fight the grasshoppers for them," Aunt Onie answered.

"Still pinching their heads off?" My mother winked at me; then she added, "Aunt Onie used to pick grasshoppers off the tomato plants. She'd pull their heads off and throw their carcasses over the fence for the chickens to eat."

"How charitable," I said under my breath, envisioning her on a Wanted poster for animal rights. She'd have grasshopper blood dripping off her fingers and a number printed across her chest.

Aunt Onie walked to the counter and spooned something green and slimy out of a mason jar. She put a blob on each of our plates. She stepped back and smiled with pride. "You're getting one of my last jars of chow-chow, too. This used to get a blue ribbon every year at the county fair, Shelby."

I was about to say no thanks when I saw my mother glaring at me again. I took the plate and dipped the edge of one fork prong into the glob. There was no way I was going to eat the stuff. It looked like something made out of grass. Instead I sipped at a spoonful of the hot soup. It wasn't bad.

"Do you want a glass for your corn bread, Shelby?" Aunt Onie crumbled a piece of corn bread into her own glass, then sprinkled salt and pepper on it. She filled the glass full of milk and took a drink, bits of corn bread dribbling at the edge of her mouth.

All those diet places promising to take off pounds don't hold a candle to being at Aunt Onie's. She'd demolish your appetite in no time.

My mother, on the other hand, was eating like crazy. You'd think she hadn't eaten in a year. In fact, I'd never seen her eat with so much enthusiasm.

I had my head down, trying to avoid seeing Aunt Onie slurp up her corn bread. I saw her fingernails, though. They were hard and yellow like seeds. And she had brown spots on her hands like you find on old apples.

She set her glass down and pushed her Dr Pepper bottle at me. "Shelby, honey, pour the rest of that beet juice into my bottle." I looked up, thinking I hadn't heard her right.

"Here, I'll do it." My mother saved me. She picked up the jar and carefully poured the remaining red brine into Aunt Onie's soda bottle. Aunt Onie swirled her bottle around, mixing the liquids into a dark bloody color, then she took a long drink.

I felt my stomach do a 180-degree turn.

"Aunt Onie doesn't waste anything," my mother remarked. "Not even tears. When we cried, she made us catch them in an empty bottle. She said she needed the water for the flowers."

"Pretty soon, the kids forgot all about crying," Aunt Onie added.

No wonder my mother hardly ever cried. She had a psychological hang-up going all the way back to childhood.

"Aren't the noodles good, Shelby?" my mother asked.

"Okay," I answered, taking another bite. It had bits of chicken in it. It was actually very tasty.

"It's noodles and tongue."

"It's what?"

Aunt Onie chuckled her weird marbles-knocking-together laugh. "I'll never forget that day your mama walked into the kitchen and saw a cow tongue lying on the counter. Screamed like all get-out."

My mother laughed with her. "Well, I didn't know people ate things like that. It was just sitting there, kind of curled up at the tip, a huge tongue, longer than your foot, Shelby. . . ."

"That's enough," I said to her, picturing a size-9 tongue lying on the counter. Now I knew I'd be sick.

"It had taste buds and everything." She wouldn't stop. "Tongue is delicious, though, if you don't think about what you're eating."

I set my spoon down. It was too late. I was thinking about it. I'd starve to death before I ate another bite in this house.

Aunt Onie chuckled again and tipped her soda bottle up. She drank the last drop and licked her lips. It was like I was at the carnival in the House of Horrors and I couldn't find my way out.

My mother had just gotten started. "And remember the time I came into the kitchen and saw that bucket on the floor, how it was full of bloody water? I saw the butcher knife on the counter, and I practically went berserk."

It seems that Aunt Onie had been out wringing chickens' necks, and she'd brought them inside to finish the butchering. Then she'd had to run back out again to check on a problem with the well. My mother had come inside, not knowing what was going on. She hadn't noticed the feathers stuck on the knife, much less the chickens on the table. She saw the bloody knife and thought someone had been murdered.

"I didn't know people had to kill chickens in order to eat them," my mother told us. "I came in and saw the blood and it scared me." As she thought about it, she quit smiling. She got quiet and it was like a shadow had passed over her face.

"You ran off and hid in the closet under the attic stairs," Aunt Onie reminded her. "I like to never found you. You were all huddled up down there, shaking like a stuck washing machine."

"And then there was that time you skinned that rattlesnake. . . ."

"Excuse me," I said, pushing my chair away from the table. "I'm not hungry." My mother glared at me for being rude. I didn't care. I'd eat one of those grasshoppers on the tomato plants before I'd hear any more sick stories or eat the tongue of anything.

I went outside and walked around back. A long time ago, the pine trees were probably planted to shield the house from the wind. They'd definitely lost the battle, I thought, gazing past their thinned-out branches.

The storm shelter lay almost in the center of the yard, a big tin door pressed into the ground. When you live in an apartment and a tornado comes, you don't have anyplace to run to. My mother says it's okay with her. She doesn't like underground cellars. They make her think she's walking into a grave.

I looked around. My mother's blackbird was buried out here somewhere. It would be just the kind of thing Georgia O'Keeffe would love, a pile of bones wearing a fake diamond earring. It'd be like her famous horse's skull, the one with the rose in its eye socket. I scared myself. Even I was starting to think about the dumb artist.

My mother says I'm the most cynical person she's ever met. Roo says it too. But she says my cynicism is my protection from a mother who has moved me around like a pawn on a chessboard. I had to build up defenses.

"Shelby!" It was my mother. She was standing at the back door hollering for me to come in.

"Come get ready for the festival!"

I looked down at my T-shirt and jeans. "I am ready," I hollered back at her. It's not like I have to dress for success at the Red Valley Sorghum Street Festival.

The screen door slammed, and I sat down under the trees, leaning against one of the thin trunks. The photograph of my father popped up in my mind like a red flag. Even when I wasn't thinking about it, it appeared as if it didn't want to let me alone. I saw his shiny belt buckle. Probably every man within two hundred miles of here had one just like it. It wasn't unusual.

Somebody in Red Valley knew the answer. I was sure of it. It was just a matter of finding out who.

Inside, my mother had finished eating. She'd put on her dressy Georgia O'Keeffe: the long black skirt with the elastic waist, a black blouse, and a white silk iris the size of a small grapefruit pinned to her chest. The thing was almost as bad as a homecoming mum. She was sitting on the couch reading an old *National Geographic.* She handed me one and said we were waiting on Aunt Onie.

"She's getting dressed up for town. She's so excited. You'd think she was going to a prom."

"Doesn't she ever go out anywhere?"

"Not much anymore. Church, I guess, if someone picks her up." She looked at my T-shirt. It says ZEUS GETS HIGH in big letters and underneath in small letters, ON OLYMPUS. It was our Latin Club fund-raiser.

"Is that what you're wearing?"

"What's wrong with it?" I knew she didn't approve. If it were up to my mother, I'd dress like Shirley Temple when she sings "The Good Ship Lollipop."

"I didn't bring anything else," I told her. That wasn't quite true, but I hadn't brought anything else I felt like changing into.

"All right," she said with a sigh. "I just hope no one gets the wrong idea."

"I'll just tell them I have a weekend pass from the drug rehab," I joked. "Lighten up. The T-shirt's antidrug, if that's what you're worried about. Zeus is high on Olympus; high, as on a ladder." You have to explain everything to my mother. She still didn't get it, though.

I sat beside her and skimmed through the *National Geographic*. It was disgusting. On one page a line of naked men paraded around with gourds on their private parts. I couldn't help but look; no one could. I saw my mother glance over at me, and I turned the page.

Just then, Aunt Onie walked in.

"Oh my g—" I slapped my hand over my mouth. It was worse than the gourds.

My mother grinned at her. "Look at you! Don't you look cute!"

She looked anything but cute. She was wearing big fat shorts that looked like a parachute and she had knee-high hose on her skinny legs. They reached halfway up on her calves, like something pathetic. Not to mention the purple sweater and the purple stripes on her sneakers.

I gave my mother a look that meant *You're not going to let her go like that, are you?*

"Zoe, honey, hand me my purse," she said. "It's under the coffee table. I need my rain cap."

I watched as my mother bent down and handed Aunt Onie a pink vinyl purse the size of a shopping bag.

"Is it supposed to rain tonight?" I asked. "Maybe we should stay in."

"My leg's been aching all day," Aunt Onie answered. "It'll rain."

She opened her purse and pulled out a folded strip of red plastic with two strings attached. She shook it and it unfolded magically like a fan. It was a rain bonnet. She placed it on her head and tied the strings under her chin, squeezing her face into a wrinkled circle, small and pinched like a rabbit's.

When we walked outside, I was glad it was almost dark. My mother led the way to the car, followed by Aunt Onie, then me. With each step, the red lights on her sneakers blinked like crazy.

"Zoe, honey, is that you?" Aunt Onie reached her arms out in front of her like a sleepwalker.

"I'm straight ahead of you, Aunt Onie."

"Oh. Straight ahead. That's where I don't see things so good."

"Grab Aunt Onie's hand, Shelby, so she won't fall and break her neck. I'll go ahead and get the car started."

I didn't want to hold her hand. It was a hand that had cut up tongues and pinched grasshoppers' heads. It had wrung the necks of innocent chickens. No telling what else it had done.

I reached for my pockets, but Aunt Onie grabbed me. Her hand felt like a claw. Suddenly it came to me that I didn't really want to find my father in a place like Red Valley. In fact, if old Georgia O'Keeffe painted my feelings, the picture would look like something squashed and moldy. Red Valley was a place that I wanted to leave as soon as possible.

Chapter Nine

THE GEORGIA O'KEEFFE CLONE AND THE RED Plastic Bonnet Lady rode in the front seat. I sat in the back with my sunglasses on. If we'd been driving down a street at home, I would have crawled onto the floorboard.

When we got downtown, the street in front of the courthouse was blocked off with sawhorses. A gazebo on wheels had been set up on the lawn, and blue Christmas lights and gold tinsel were woven in and out of the lattices. A big megaphonelike speaker boomed out country music.

The whole town must have come, because there were pickups and cars down all the side streets. We parked and got out, my mother in her artist's designer clothes, Aunt Onie in her cartoon designer clothes. I walked a few feet behind them, still wearing my sunglasses. I'd pretend I had an eye disease.

The first person I recognized was Reese, the guy I'd met in the drugstore that morning. He still had on his cowboy outfit and his butter-dish belt buckle and a toothpick in the side of his mouth. He walked right up to Aunt Onie.

"How're your angels doing, Miss Purdy?" he asked, grinning. "Still sending people to you?"

She smiled and nodded her red plastic head.

Reese moved his toothpick to the other side of his mouth and squinted at me. "Somethin' the matter with your eyes, Shelby?"

He was making fun of my sunglasses, of course. There are times you just want to disappear.

We headed toward the gazebo, where Teena was supposed to perform.

"Y'all going to eat?" he asked. Up ahead were barbecue grills made out of big black barrels. The smoke mixed into the air and it smelled wonderful. I was starving. I'd had only one noodle and a teeny bite of tongue.

"We already ate," Aunt Onie announced. "Shelby here fell in love with my chow-chow and tongue soup. That girl can eat!" I was about to protest, but my mother gave me one of her looks that said *Don't say a word*.

Reese walked past us to get a plate, and we went on toward the picnic tables. The elms in front of the courthouse were decorated in lights. They were pretty. It looked like tiny white stars had fallen into the branches. The building behind them, though, like so much in this town, was dark and empty. Lines of sparrows sat on the vacant window ledges like eyelashes on a dead person.

We sat down at one of the tables.

"Aunt Onie, how long has the courthouse been gone?" my mother asked. "Empty, I mean."

"It caught fire a few years ago," she responded. "Everybody's records got burned. We just closed it up."

I wondered if my birth certificate had been there. A few weeks ago, when I needed it for driver's ed, my mother said she couldn't find it.

She stared at the burned-out courthouse. "One of the doors, I remember, was so beautiful. It had carvings on it, like those pictures you see in medieval art books."

"Why don't you walk up there and look around?" I told her. "I'll stay and keep Aunt Onie company."

When she left, I'd tell Aunt Onie about the photograph. Maybe, if I got lucky, she'd know something.

My mother stood up. At that exact moment, a voice screeched at us.

"Hi, y'all!" It was Teena, running toward us in a shiny gold cowgirl outfit and gold spiked heels. A little boy dressed up like Superman ran with her.

"R.J.! You stepped on Mama's new shoes!" Teena stopped in front of us, out of breath.

"I'm not R.J. I'm Superman, of course."

"This outfit cost me fifty dollars and I had to pay twenty-five to get these heels dyed gold." Teena pulled off one shoe and examined it.

R.J. cocked his head and looked at his mother. He held the remains of a candy apple in one hand, and his face was covered in sticky caramel. Suddenly, he threw his arms around her and kissed her. At the same time, his cape caught the edge of an iced-tea glass on our table. It dumped down the front of her outfit.

She screamed. Superman flew off, wiping out everything in his path. Teena stood there with her arms spread out, staring at the big wet puddle of iced tea running down the front of her gold satin jeans. She stomped her foot. Then she looked up at the gazebo.

"What the . . . !" she shrieked. Someone had backed a van up to the stage. A large woman in a white pantsuit was unloading a big wooden horse on wheels. It looked like a huge pull-toy.

"They were supposed to bring me a cardboard horse from the movie theater, one of those that stands up. It was supposed to be realistic!"

She was just about to cry as Reese returned carrying his plate. He tried to explain it to her.

"It's our Trojan horse from school; we built it for one of our plays last year. It's really cool. You can open up the stomach, even ride inside it."

Teena didn't want to hear about it. *Trojan* to her meant practically nothing. It sure didn't mean a horse that cowboys ride.

"I didn't pay that kind of money for my outfit to have to perform with a Trojan . . . whatever . . . that thing!" She crossed her arms across her chest and pouted.

Reese turned and waved at the woman on the stage who was busy tying a red bandanna around the horse's neck. "That's our drama teacher," he told me.

"And that there's my stage prop?" Teena still couldn't believe it.

"It's not that bad," Reese said.

"Yes, it is that bad," Teena pouted. "It's the number one most ridiculous thing I ever laid eyes on. My career is practically going down the drain this very minute."

The woman onstage squatted down to open a door cut into the horse's stomach. The small fuzzy head of a cat poked out.

"Oh, no." Teena put her face in her hands and bawled. "She brought the cats. This is not what I had in mind at all!"

Just then, the woman in the white pantsuit stepped off the stage and walked toward us. Under each arm she carried a cat wearing a tiny cowboy hat covered in blue glitter. They looked like Dallas Cowboy cheerleaders.

"Hi, Reese. Hello, Miss Purdy, Teena." Then she spoke to Aunt Onie. "You have company, I see."

Aunt Onie nodded. "Hello, Annabelle Wynette. Yes, these girls, Shelby and Zoe, come all this way to spend a week with me."

I stiffened. "Two days," I corrected.

"Annabelle Wynette Sloan," the woman said, holding out her hand first to my mother and then to me. "I'm glad to meet you. Reese probably told you I teach drama at the high school. He's the best set builder in the state. He plays a decent Ferdinand, too."

I couldn't believe Red Valley would have its own high school, much less a drama department. And Ferdinand was a character in *The Tempest*, a Shakespeare play we'd read in the fall. Reese looked like a bull rider, not an actor.

"Let me introduce Calpurnia and Portia," Annabelle said proudly, holding the cats up for us to see. "They're going to meow 'Home on the Range.' " She looked at Teena. "They're your lead-in act, but I need you to go up there with them."

"With the ca-ats?" Teena looked horrified.

"They know what to do when I turn on the tape," Annabelle was saying. "But you may have to help them out some."

"Do *what*?"

"You know, meow a little, to get them started. You do know the tune, don't you?"

"If you think I'm going to stand up onstage and meow in front of everyone, I'm quitting right now!" Suddenly she looked around. R.J. was gone.

"*Superman!*" she hollered across the lawn.

"I'm right here, of course," came a small voice from under the table. "I need to go to the bathroom, of course."

"I'll take him," Reese volunteered.

Teena reluctantly followed Annabelle toward the stage.

"You should have seen the Fourth of July parade last summer," Aunt Onie remarked. "Annabelle Wynette built a Statue of Liberty out of chicken wire. She sprayed it silver and put it on one of those little red wagons. The kitties wore red, white, and blue vests with stars and little black three-cornered hats. Everybody around here loved it."

"Where we come from people don't dress up their cats."

She ignored me. "She's got those two cats, plus Miranda, Katharina, Lady Macbeth, and Ophelia." She counted on her crooked fingers. "Oh, and Titania. Some people around here call her the Cat Lady." She smiled proudly in Annabelle's direction.

Reese returned with R.J. and sat down with us.

R.J. put his elbows on the table and rested his chin in his hands. Reese's food was probably cold, but he didn't complain.

"Want to try some calf fries, Shelby?" He pointed to some fried things piled on his plate. The pieces looked a lot like clam strips.

"Sure," I said, reaching for one.

He grinned while I took a bite and chewed. It had an odd texture.

"What did you say these were?"

Aunt Onie bent over and whispered in my ear.

I thought I was going to be sick. What I heard was something no one would want to hear, especially from an elderly lady. It made it even more gross. My mother bit her lip. Then she burst out laughing.

It wasn't funny. Eating the tongue of something was one thing. Eating its private parts was a million times worse, especially when they were fried to look like clam strips.

Aunt Onie sat there grinning. She still had her rain bonnet tied under her chin. She looked like a Cabbage Patch doll.

Reese said he was sorry, that he thought I knew what calf fries were. Right, as if people in civilized parts of the United States ate the things.

"Let's go on over to the stage," my mother said cheerfully. "We'll find a spot on the grass to sit."

"I have a hard time getting up from down-low places," Aunt Onie remarked. "Maybe I'll just stay right here at the table."

"I heard you climbed up on the water tower one time," Reese said. "It was before I was born."

"Lordy, yes," Aunt Onie said, laughing. "I was young then, not much more than seventy."

"Georgia O'Keeffe," my mother began, forgetting all about her promise not to talk about her, "used to sit on her roof. She was in her seventies, at least. She had this ladder attached to her house."

Reese listened politely. R.J. was under the table digging a hole with a plastic spoon. He was planting a watermelon seed.

"Georgia O'Keeffe," Aunt Onie mused. "I met her one time. Of course, I was just a little girl."

My mother looked up, startled. She got so excited, she was practically breaking out in hives. "You met *the* Georgia O'Keeffe? The artist?"

Aunt Onie nodded.

"Mama took me over to the college in Canyon. Miss O'Keeffe was teaching there at the time, and my mama was taking a class in education. It was, let's see, during the war, must've been around 1916 or '17."

"I can't believe you met Georgia O'Keeffe!" My mother was shaking her head incredulously. You'd think she'd just found out Aunt Onie was the one who invented toilet paper.

"Miss O'Keeffe lived in the college president's house," Aunt Onie explained. "It was a big white two-story house on the campus. People thought she was odd. They said she went out with men unchaperoned, took walks by herself in the canyon. They said she refused to teach out of any of the regular art books, had to do things her own way."

My mother's face was flushed as she listened.

Aunt Onie went on. "Miss O'Keeffe wasn't particularly friendly. You'd call her hard, I guess. But for some reason she noticed me, a skinny little girl sitting on the library steps at the college. I was waiting for my mother."

"What did she say to you?" My mother was biting her bottom lip, waiting.

"Well sir, she bent down and said, 'You're an artist, aren't you?' "

Aunt Onie pressed her lips into a thin smile. "I told her I wanted to be a wood-carver. Of course, in those days everybody said carving was for the men and boys. Women should only use knives for cutting up carrots. Miss O'Keeffe looked so pleased. She said, 'Listen to yourself.' "

Aunt Onie smiled. "When we got home, Mama told Daddy. He went straight out and bought me a piano, not a knife! Later on, the tornado got the piano.

Still don't know how it got out the window. I suspect the wind just sucked it out." She stopped and chuckled at the memory.

My mother fingered the iris on her blouse. She was thinking about Georgia O'Keeffe, I'm sure, but the tornado was on Aunt Onie's mind.

She stopped talking and sniffed the air. "I smell that rain coming."

"Is that all?" my mother asked. "Did she say anything else. Or do anything?"

"Well, yes," Aunt Onie remembered, tightening the strings on her rain bonnet. "She did do one other thing. She gave me a little drawing. I still have it somewhere."

My mother jumped up. "Do you think you could find it, Aunt Onie? Do you really think it's still around?"

Aunt Onie tried to explain that the picture wasn't much, just a few sketchy lines on a small piece of paper, but my mother didn't care. It was a dream come true. She grabbed up Superman and danced around the table with him. I thought I'd die, and Reese could probably tell.

"Want to go sit on the grass?" he asked me. I was glad to have an excuse to leave.

We walked off toward one of the elms, away from the crowd. I sat down and Reese stretched out on his back beside me. He rested his hat over his eyes as if he were sleeping. I looked at him. He wore a white Western shirt, starched jeans, and black cowboy boots.

His belt was black too, with silver trim, the buckle silver with gold around the edges, the kind of buckle cowboys win at rodeos. I felt myself shiver inside.

Maybe it was because I'd never seen a boy so close. I looked at him lying there, his shirt open at his neck, his fancy belt. I saw all of him.

I pulled my knees up to my chest and wrapped my arms tight around my legs. I looked up into the tree. Its thick branches moved in the wind, making the leaves quiver.

Onstage, Teena had started singing with the cats, her lead-in act. She had a kitty under each arm. " 'Where seldom is heard a discouraging word, and the skies are not cloudy all day . . .' "

The song ended with a huge clap of thunder. A drop of rain hit my arm, and Superman bounded up onstage, his cape ballooning in the wind. Teena hadn't even gotten to start her part of the act. Suddenly the rain gushed down like an avalanche.

"Come get under the gazebo," Annabelle hollered. Pretty soon we were all up there, Teena, R.J., my mother, Aunt Onie, Reese and I, and a whole lot of other people. Aunt Onie looked around proudly in her plastic rain bonnet, the only one prepared for a storm.

It stopped almost as soon as it had started, but everyone had already packed up to leave. Teena's singing career hadn't gotten past the first raindrop.

"Y'all leaving for home tomorrow?" she asked glumly.

"Yes," I answered. My mother was strangely quiet.

On the way back to the house, it hit me that I hadn't even thought about the photograph. With everything going on, I hadn't had a chance to ask Aunt Onie. Roo says when you really don't want to do something, deep down, you forget about it. She says you do it to protect yourself.

Tomorrow I'd ask Aunt Onie, no matter what. Before we left Red Valley, I'd find out the truth.

Chapter Ten

MY MOTHER WANTED THAT GEORGIA O'KEEFFE drawing. It was all she could think about. Aunt Onie promised she'd look for it first thing in the morning, but my mother could hardly wait and went straight to bed, hoping the night would pass faster. It was like Christmas Eve, there was so much tension in the air.

Me, I went outside and sat on the porch. The night was quiet and cool. Aunt Onie's window was open, and I could hear her shuffling around, getting ready for bed.

After a while I heard a scratching on the window screen. Then I heard her calling me. "Shelby, come here, please."

I waited, pretending not to hear; then she called me again. I got up and went inside. Aunt Onie was sitting up in bed. She'd unraveled her braids, and her white hair hung in crinkles like icicles down her back and shoulders. She reached her hand up to me.

"Come closer, dear."

"I'm still kind of wet."

"That's all right."

I moved in a few inches, but I stood away from the edge of the bed.

Her hand shook as she pulled a strand of hair away from her mouth.

"You think I'm a crazy old woman who don't know much."

I didn't know what to say. "Not really," I lied.

"Do you hear the wind?"

It had died down, making a soft shooshing sound.

"That's the kind of pain your mama has. Sometimes it dies down low, then it picks up again."

In the dark Aunt Onie looked like the shadow of something pretty. I felt uneasy at what she was saying. My mother wasn't in any kind of pain that I knew about.

"She just wants to go to New Mexico," I said. "It's like this big dream she has." It was a dumb thing to say, but it was all I could think of.

"The promised land," Aunt Onie whispered. She lay back, resting a thin wrist across her forehead. "She thinks it's waiting for her. Now that everything's over."

"What's over?" I asked, but she didn't say a word. Aunt Onie wasn't making any sense again. This confirmed it. She was senile. She pulled the sheet up under her chin, and closed her eyes.

I opened the curtain and walked out. The Christmas lights on the mantel in the living room and the Santa light in the window had been unplugged, so the room was dark. I gently opened the door of the bedroom where my mother was sleeping. She looked fine to me.

I eased the door shut and tiptoed away.

In the middle of the night, it stormed again. One minute the sky was ripping apart, the next it was quiet. I kept waiting for the sound of a train, which is what tornadoes are supposed to sound like.

I waited for a long time.

It was the square of light that woke me up. The sun was shining through the window, making a small yellow patch on my bed. Then I remembered. We were going home. I got up, packed my things, and headed downstairs.

My mother was sitting at the kitchen table dipping her tea bag in and out of her cup. She had her calendar pages in front of her on the table and was looking at a painting called *Black Place*. It's a gray hill that used to be smooth, but it's split apart in the middle. Something like poison drips down the black part between the halves. Georgia O'Keeffe must have painted it when she was having a bad day.

"Aunt Onie can't find the drawing."

"Oh," I said, feeling her disappointment seep into me.

"I almost had it, too. I came that close!" She put her thumb and finger together, measuring a tiny distance.

It might as well have been a million miles. It was all the same; she didn't have the drawing. It probably got burned in the trash years ago. I didn't try to explain that to my mother, though. She looked too sad.

"I'm sorry." I really was. I even thought about trying to draw something, signing "G.O'K." at the bottom. Aunt Onie had plenty of old paper. I doubted I could fool my mother, though.

"It's okay, I guess," she said, sighing. "Anyway, I had another dream. Want to see it?" She flipped past *Black Place* to another calendar page.

It was a ladder, floating in a greenish blue sky.

"Where's Aunt Onie?" Even though I felt sorry for my mother, I didn't feel like getting into a discussion about one of her dreams. No telling where we'd wind up.

"She's outside carving. But look at this painting. And eat something."

"What's that?" I asked, looking at a jar of lumpy yellow stuff on the table.

She didn't even look up. "Homemade pear jam. Try some." She pushed the jar toward me.

"No, thanks." I picked up a plain biscuit and took a bite.

My mother rested her elbows on the table with her chin in her hands. "Anyway, this was in my dream last night, Shelby."

"The ladder or the pear jam?"

"The ladder, silly. You know that cedar chest at the end of my bed? I woke up and Georgia O'Keeffe was standing on it. She was wearing the same black dress she wore in the first dream."

"Doesn't even bother to change clothes between dreams!" I joked. I got up and walked to the counter to pour myself a cup of coffee. It was strong and black, the way I like it. I was thinking about the coffee when my mother stood up on the kitchen chair. She raised her arms into the air.

"Georgia O'Keeffe was standing there like this. Then all of a sudden a ladder appeared. It hung in the air between the floor and the ceiling, not touching anything."

"Did she mention that you hadn't picked up any bones yet?"

"Shelby, I'm not joking. No, she didn't *say* anything. When the ladder appeared, she left."

"Okay, I'll interpret it. We're supposed to climb up into our car and head back home."

My mother was thinking. She dipped her spoon into the jam and ate a lump right out of the jar. "The painting is called *The Ladder to the Moon*. It suggests something . . . I don't know . . . something outside this world, I suppose."

I looked over her shoulder at the painting. Besides the suspended ladder, there was a tiny half moon at the top of the page and an edge of black hills at the bottom. It was better than *Black Place*, at least.

She went on to explain. "In my dream, or whatever, I didn't see the moon. But the ladder was so real, Shelby. It's got to mean something! Ladders . . . let's see," she thought out loud. "They . . . connect things."

"Like highways connect places on the map!" I said, getting up. "It's a sign! We should leave!"

She laughed at me, then got up from the table, saying she had some things to pack.

If I hurried, I could get the photograph from my journal and show Aunt Onie. Just as I got up from the table, though, I heard something terrible.

It was a long, quivery cry like something in a nightmare. I ran out of the kitchen toward the back door, where the sound had come from.

Aunt Onie was standing at the door. Her face was grayish white. Then I saw the blood spurting from her palm like a fountain. I yelled for my mother.

"Hold your arm up, Aunt Onie!" I said, running toward her.

The blood that poured from her hand had streamed to her elbow, and it dripped onto the floor in a pool. I'd never seen anyone bleed so fast or so much. Quickly I placed my fingers on the deepest part of the gash. It stretched between her thumb and forefinger into the palm of her hand. Applying as much pressure as I could, I yelled again for my mother.

Finally she walked in from the bedroom.

"How many times have I asked you not to yell for me. Come to me when you— Oh . . . no!"

"Get a towel from the bathroom," I shouted. "There aren't any bandages or anything." I remembered the medicine cabinet. This would take more than Aunt Onie's Monkey Blood and Band-Aids.

"All I want is ice," Aunt Onie whimpered, leaning against me. "Just get me some ice, Zoe. My mouth is so dry."

"I'm Shelby, Aunt Onie." The blood seeped through my fingers as I pressed harder into the wound.

My mother returned with one of the thin pink towels from the bathroom. I tied it tightly around Aunt Onie's hand.

"I'll keep pressure on it while you drive," I told my mother. "The cut doesn't really look so bad. I don't know why it's bleeding so much."

"Is the clinic still downtown?" my mother asked Aunt Onie.

Aunt Onie opened and shut her mouth like a dying fish.

"Sweetie, is the clinic—"

"You know it is, Zoe," Aunt Onie whined. "You've been there."

"Her skin's cold," I said. "She might be in shock. Grab that afghan in the living room and let's go."

We wrapped Aunt Onie in the afghan and the two of us carried her to the car, setting her between us in the front seat. On the way, I continued applying pressure to the cut.

I looked down at Aunt Onie's feet. Her shoes were untied, and her feet were swollen, stuffed into them like bread dough that's risen over the side of the pan.

I wondered if she might be dying. I hugged her up closer to keep her warm.

Chapter Eleven

THE WAITING ROOM AT THE CLINIC WAS EMPTY except for the receptionist, a white-haired lady who sat perched on a stool. She was dressed in a black-and-white pantsuit. She looked like a penguin.

"Excuse me," my mother said.

The Penguin Lady peered over the top of her glasses at Aunt Onie.

"Good morning, Miss Purdy. Uh-oh. What'd you go and do to your hand? Carving again?" She clucked her tongue against the roof of her mouth and slowly lifted herself off the stool. At the same time, she reached inside her dress to pull up one of her bra straps.

"Please, hurry!" My mother's voice sounded high-pitched and strained.

The Penguin Lady sighed loudly; then she turned and hollered like someone calling in a hamburger order in a cafe. "Dr. Sam! Stitch-up!" She cocked her head to listen.

The doctor emerged from behind a pink-curtained door, pushing a wheelchair. She extended her hand to my mother and nodded at me. "Samantha Woodridge. What do we have here?"

Aunt Onie folded up into the chair and the three of them disappeared into a back room.

I went to the rest room and washed my hands. The blood flowed down the drain in a pale red stream, and as I watched it, I felt sick to my stomach. I used another squirt of soap and washed again. When I came out, I sat down in one of the chairs in the waiting room and picked up a magazine. I was perfectly calm. Then all of a sudden my hands were shaking like crazy.

"You okay?"

I felt the Penguin Lady looking at me with those small round penguin eyes. I told her I was fine and I started reading dumb stuff just to hold my mind still. I'd just begun an article about making no-fat pizza dough out of cauliflower when she spoke to me again.

"Was that your mama with Miss Purdy?" She chewed on the end of a pencil eraser while she thought. "She sure does look familiar somehow."

I answered that she was my mother and went back to my reading.

"That's riiight," she said slowly, stretching the word out like a piece of bubble gum. She removed her glasses and let them dangle on the chain around her neck. "I believe I met your mama years ago. She hasn't changed that much. Cute little thing. We thought for sure she'd gone into labor early. Must've been pregnant with you."

"You might have her mixed up with someone else. I wasn't born here."

"Hmmm, maybe, but . . ." She put her glasses back on and thought. "No, it's her, I'm sure of it. What's your mama's given name?"

"Zoe."

"Yep. I remembered it was something odd. She come in here with Miss Purdy and a feller. He was all worried about her. She'd fallen down the cellar steps, and she was bruised up pretty good. She was having contractions, real erratic-like. What's your daddy's name?"

My insides felt loose, like a pile of rubber bands, but I said "Neil," one of my favorite astronaut names. I used to imagine it printed on his NASA uniform.

"Nope." She shook her head. "Wadn't anything like Neil. The guy I'm thinking of had a funny name, like Doody, or something. Howdy Doody." She stopped and laughed at herself.

"No, honey, that was a TV show," she said, mostly to herself. She laughed again and dug around in her purse. She brought up a lipstick pencil and a compact and drew two red peaks just above the edge of her top lip. "Guess you're too young to remember the *Howdy Doody* show. That was long before your time."

At that point, my mother pushed Aunt Onie into the waiting room in a wheelchair, Dr. Sam walking beside her.

"Is this who we need to thank?" the doctor said, extending her hand to me. "Your putting pressure on the wound kept her from bleeding to death."

Aunt Onie sat in the wheelchair with her knees spread apart and her shoes untied. Her eyes looked like melted ice cream.

"Keep that hand up, Miss Purdy." The doctor raised Aunt Onie's bandaged hand to an upright position. The blood on the front of her dress had turned brown and her new white sneakers were splattered with blood.

"Now, Miss Purdy, remember. No more carving," the doctor warned. She pulled my mother to the side and whispered, "Hide the knives. Next time, we might not be so lucky." Then Dr. Sam spoke to me. "She's going to need some help for a few days. The bandage has to be changed daily. Pour peroxide over the wound and watch for any redness or unusual heat emanating from it. I'll take the stitches out in about a week."

"A week?" I blurted.

Dr. Sam smiled. "Don't worry, Shelby. I know you're worried about your aunt, but she'll be fine."

She's not my aunt. We're not even related. And of course she'll be fine. She pulled the heads off grasshoppers and chopped up cow tongues. I'm the one who isn't fine. I'm the one who has to get out of here, to go home.

As soon as we got in the car Aunt Onie fell asleep, her cut hand propped up against my shoulder like a stop sign.

"The doctor said the reason she bled so much was because of the heart medication she's been on," my mother explained as she started up the car. "It's got a blood thinner in it. I hate to think what might have happened, Shelby, if we hadn't been there."

Aunt Onie would have bled to death. Still, the fact that she was alive caused even more problems.

We'd have to stay longer. Then I felt bad for thinking such a thought.

Maybe Teena would know someone who could change Aunt Onie's bandages, stay with her a few days.

"Can we stop at the drugstore?" I asked. I told my mother what I was thinking.

She headed down the block and pulled up to the curb in front of the drugstore.

I looked down at Aunt Onie. Her body pressed hard against me, in a deep sleep. I'd have to wait in the car with her; she'd fall over if I got out.

"I'll go in," my mother said. "I'll talk to Teena, and I'll get the peroxide and the swabs. We have gauze, don't we?"

I said yes. The doctor had given us a whole box, along with some pain pills, antibiotics, and medicated ointment.

After she left, I looked out the window. The bench my mother had slept on before I was born was still there. It's funny how things like that last, but it had. I tried to imagine her lying on it. She'd be resting on her side, probably, her knees drawn up under her. She would have her sweater folded under her head for a pillow. No, not her sweater. It was winter. She'd be wearing the sweater. Maybe she'd have her purse under her head.

Or maybe her head was in his lap. Maybe he had his hand on her hair, pushing it away from her face. I saw him sitting there, his boots, the silver tips, the jeans, the silver buckle. I looked inside myself and tried to see his face. Then I remembered. He wouldn't have been sitting on the bench. Aunt Onie had said my mother had been alone that night.

I laid my head back on the edge of the car seat and shut my eyes.

"I'm back!" It was my mother. She scooted into the car, tossing me a box of Luden's cherry cough drops. It was a bad sign. I used to beg for the things when I was a kid. It meant she hadn't gotten anyone to stay with Aunt Onie.

"So who's coming out to keep her?" I asked the question anyway. Roo says you should always think positively. She says positive thoughts drive out the negative, so that good things can happen.

"Nobody's coming out to keep her. Just us."

She turned on the radio. Some whiny person who sounded a whole lot like Teena was singing at the top of her lungs about kissing somebody on a pool table.

"You didn't even ask Teena, did you?"

"I'm not leaving her, Shelby. I can't." She started the car.

"You're crazy!" I raised my voice. "I told Roo we'd be back. And what about your job?"

"Shhh," my mother warned, nodding at Aunt Onie. "I called Rosie. She said not to worry. Plus she said she'd advance me some cash."

"How much longer?" I whispered.

"Just a few days. You'll be back in time for school."

The loose ends of Aunt Onie's hair fuzzed out in a web around her face. She looked really old, like something ancient dragged up from the ocean floor, but her eyelids were thin and bluish like a baby's.

She slept, breathing in quiet even puffs. I turned off the radio. There was nothing I could do.

Roo says I'm just like Phoebe, Holden's sister in *The Catcher in the Rye*. She says Phoebe put up with too much and that I do too. I tried to think, to imagine what Roo would tell me to do. I had some money.

I knew I couldn't leave. There had to be someone responsible to hold things down, to make sure Aunt Onie got doctored and fed.

When we got to the house, I tied Aunt Onie's sneakers; then we helped her out of the car and inside.

"Shelby, you get her situated," my mother said. "I'll check the kitchen and see what we're going to need from the grocery store. I'll get some potato chips, some things you like." She was placating again. I knew because I'd used the word *placating* fifty times last month to get my extra credit in English.

Aunt Onie wanted to sit in the corner of the couch, so I led her there and got her settled. Then she wanted her afghan, and it had to be the yellow-and-orange one, which took a while to find. After that, she had to have her Dr Pepper. The floor fan had to be turned on, and the window blinds had to be opened so that she could look out at the birds sitting on the sawhorse outside. Finally, she wanted a dip of snuff.

She must not have seen the film I'd seen in health. A guy's entire lip rotted out; it looked like road-kill, but I didn't argue with her. She told me where to look in the kitchen, under the counter inside an oat-meal box.

I handed the snuffbox to her with a short warning about the cancer it could cause, but she didn't listen. She pinched a lump between her fingers and stuffed it inside her bottom lip. She sucked on it and rubbed her tongue against her teeth.

"Shelby?" she said as I was about to leave the room.

I stopped. *Now what.*

With her good hand, she reached into the pocket in her dress.

"Here, honey. You'll have to finish this." She handed me a bloodstained lump of wood. "I was making it for you, remember?" Her words were slurred, either from the medication or the snuff, I wasn't sure which.

I've never carved anything, unless you want to count a bar of Ivory soap. That was in the third grade and the whole class made the same thing, an open book. The teacher lined all twenty-nine soap books on the windowsills for the parents to see at open house. Then we all went home and took a bath.

Aunt Onie pointed at a place on the wood. "You'll have to carve it," she answered. "See? One wing's just about out." She touched the bloodiest part, where you could see feathers coming out of the wood. "You can't leave it in there, honey. Here, take it."

"Okay," I agreed. But I wasn't taking up wood carving. I'm not the Teenage Wood-Carving Champion of the World type. I'd throw the thing in a field on the way out of town, and she'd never know the difference.

That afternoon while Aunt Onie slept, my mother dug in cabinets and drawers trying to find the O'Keeffe drawing Aunt Onie had talked about. She was rummaging through the rolltop desk when I approached her.

"Who was the man with you?" I asked.

She squeezed her eyebrows together like she didn't know what I was talking about.

"At the clinic," I added, "when you were pregnant with me. The receptionist said you'd fallen down the cellar steps and gotten bruised up. She said my father brought you in."

She looked at me, startled. Then she frowned. She shook her head slowly and I thought she was going to finally admit it. The man who brought her into the clinic was my father.

"Shelby, the man she was talking about was a neighbor, a friend of Aunt Onie's. He drove me to the clinic. I had tripped. The stairs are so hard; they're made out of cement, and my being pregnant I was off-balance and I caught my heel—"

I interrupted her. The details about the fall weren't important. "You're saying my father wasn't with you at the clinic?"

"No. I mean yes, that's what I'm saying. Let it go. It's over."

I ran upstairs, closed the door, and sat on the bed. It was time. I had to show her the photograph. I slid it from the pages of my journal and went back downstairs.

"Here!" I shoved it at her. "It's not over!"

She froze, her face turning bright red. Then she exploded. "You got into my room! You were going through my things!"

"Who is it?" I strained to make my voice louder than hers. "Or are you just going to make up another lie like you've always done? Go ahead, lie! Lie!"

The color drained from her face. "Don't talk to me like that. The photograph is nothing. I can explain, but now is not a good time, not while you're so angry."

"It's never a good time for you! I knew that's what you'd say. I'm moving in with Roo. Her parents want me to have a normal life. They want to pay for my lunches; they want—"

"Enough, Shelby!" she shot back. She turned, walked to her room, and slammed the door. I picked up the photograph from the floor, where she'd dropped it.

She stayed in her room the rest of the day. I had to make Aunt Onie's lunch and give her the antibiotics and painkillers. I had to find her an empty tin can for her to spit her snuff into, and I had to help her dress. She wanted me to put her bloody clothes in a tub of cold water, so I had to do that, too. I also wrote Roo a long letter.

I told her I wasn't moving around anymore, that if her parents really didn't mind, I'd like to move in with them. I'd get a part-time job and help out with expenses. I folded the letter and put it inside my journal. There comes a time when you have to assume responsibility for yourself.

In the late afternoon Reese came by.

"Hi," he said, standing at the doorway holding a paper grocery sack. "We heard about Miss Purdy's accident. My mom cooked a couple of meals."

I thanked him and he followed me into the kitchen.

"Where is everybody?" he asked. The house was as quiet as a tomb.

"Asleep," I answered. "Aunt Onie's doped up. My mother's . . . I guess she's just tired. She's in her room."

After we put everything away, we each got a Dr Pepper and went back outside on the porch. We sat in the swing and talked a little.

"How'd you get here?" I didn't see a car or truck anywhere.

"Horseback. We're only about a mile north of here."

Roo wouldn't believe it. People still used horses for transportation. It was totally medieval.

"I'd ask you to go for a ride," he said, "but I have to get back. To my dad, spring break means spring work. He's got me repairing fences. But tomorrow I've got the day off. Do you want to go out to the canyon?"

He was talking about Georgia O'Keeffe's hangout, the red whirlpool I'd torn off of our bathroom wall.

I didn't know if I wanted to go or not.

"Annabelle said she'd drive us down there. She thinks she owes me something for helping out with the sets in drama."

"The Cat Lady?"

Reese laughed. "Right. The one with the cats. So do you want to go? We could rent some horses. It's a great way to see everything. Do you like to ride?"

I said I liked riding okay. Of course, I'd never been on a real horse, but I didn't tell him that.

"We'll stop by tomorrow morning sometime. Dress grubby."

I walked with him around to the back, where he'd tied up his horse to one of the pine tree trunks. He untied her and swung up on her back.

"See you tomorrow, Shelby!" he called out as he rode off.

By suppertime, my mother still hadn't come out of her room. It was okay. I didn't feel like talking to her, either.

Aunt Onie shuffled noiselessly back and forth between her bedroom and the kitchen, her pink scuffs patting across the floor. Her routine had been messed up by getting hurt, and she seemed almost at loose ends, as if she didn't quite know what to do with herself. She tried to sleep, but if she accidentally hit her hand against the bed or touched it in any way, she awoke again, and she'd get out of bed and walk around. Finally, I led her to the kitchen and made her sit down.

I made her a cup of warm milk and heated up the soup that Reese had brought. I sliced some cheese and found a box of crackers. I had to help her eat, spooning the soup into her mouth. Finally, I gave her another dose of antibiotics and pain medication and led her to bed. I helped her rest her sore hand on a stack of pillows and told her to go to sleep.

I ate by myself. Then, while I was stacking the dishes in the sink, I remembered Aunt Onie's clothes. They were still soaking in the bathtub.

Her dress lay submerged in a thin layer of pink water. I stood at the doorway, feeling a strange panic sweep over me. It was just a dress with blood on it, nothing to be afraid of. Slowly, I knelt against the tub, wringing out the dress, trying to ignore the sadness I was feeling.

That night I slept restlessly, thinking about my mother, about the photograph. In the middle of the night, I woke up. The face of my wristwatch made a blue circle in the dark. It was 3:00 A.M.

I tiptoed down the stairs and peeked around the corner into the living room. The room was dark except for the thin yellow light that came from the porch and shined through the crack in the drapes at the picture window.

My mother sat on the floor cross-legged, hugging a pillow up next to her chest. She didn't see me. I was about to walk in when I saw that she was crying; sobbing is more like it. She was doing it without making a sound, like she was holding her breath.

I knew I should sit down beside her, put my arm around her shoulders. I didn't. I was tired of things not being right.

If you took all the shoulds of your life and stacked them to the sky, they wouldn't end, probably. They would go straight up past the clouds to who knows where. Slowly I stepped backward so the floor-boards wouldn't squeak and went back up to my room.

I lay awake in bed for a long time wondering what was going to happen. I'd finally shown her the photograph, but I knew it wasn't over. We were at the edge of a storm. I felt it coming, and I pulled the quilt up around me and tried to sleep.

Chapter Twelve

THE NOTE SAID, "WE'VE GONE TO THE cemetery." I found it on the bottom step when I came down the attic stairs to get the door.

Somebody was banging.

It was Reese.

"Do you know you have your pajamas on?"

I looked down. I was wearing my Tweety Bird pajamas, the ones I'd gotten for the beach trip. I'd forgotten all about the trip to the canyon.

"Were you still asleep?"

"Have you had an IQ test lately?" I didn't really say it, but I wanted to. I mumbled something and excused myself. I ran back upstairs.

One glance in the mirror told me my hair looked like the "before" picture in a makeover ad. I dressed quickly, brushed my teeth, and opened the door again, starting over.

Before I had a chance to say anything to Reese, Superman leaped up between us.

"Where did you come from?" I asked.

"K-marton."

"It's Krypton."

He must have been up for hours, jumping around in his Superman outfit like a loose water hose. In one hand he carried a bow, in the other, an arrow, and he had a cardboard pirate's hat on his head. He looked dangerous.

"Hi, Shelf-by," he said, grinning up at me.

"It's Shelby." He was annoying.

I looked out. Teena was coming through the gate, carrying something covered in a white dish towel. Beyond her, Annabelle Sloan emerged from the front seat of her van holding a small white cat. Everyone had shown up at once.

Annabelle looked worn out. Her blond hair frizzed out around her ears and she had grass stains on her white stirrup pants.

She started talking before she even got up to the porch. "White's supposed to be the thing this year—if you're a size three and you don't have to wallow around on the grass. It has been a morning! Hello, Shelby. Reese says you're going out to the canyon with him. Well, I'm not in any big hurry to leave, are you?"

I'd suddenly decided not to go, but she didn't give me a chance to answer. She held the cat up to me so that its eyes were level with mine. "This is Ophelia. Tell Shelby hello," she cooed.

Ophelia gave me a totally disgusted look, like I was the Quasimodo of the cat kingdom.

Annabelle kept talking. "I'm entering this kitty calendar contest," she said. "You have to take a different photograph for each month. I was trying to get everybody dressed in their July Fourth outfits for the July shoot, but they wouldn't cooperate. Finally I had to call Teena and get her to come over and help me."

Teena sniggered. "When I got there all the cats, except Ophelia, were in time-out in the garage. Annabelle was sprawled out on the grass."

"Lady Macbeth and Titania think they should be treated like queens," Annabelle said. "Ophelia, though, is a sweetie."

She gave the cat a little kiss on the lips. "This little lady knows how to behave. She needs to teach her sisters some man—" She was about to say *manners*, but Superman bounced up and just about knocked her down.

"Beeee still!" Teena scolded. "Geezy peezy, I'd like to have a nickel for every time I've said that." She looked at me. "Where's Miss Onie and your mama?"

I said they'd gone to the cemetery.

Teena didn't seem surprised. For Red Valley, the cemetery must be a normal form of entertainment.

She pushed her way into the house, followed by the rest. They went straight to the kitchen.

"This here's a tuna casserole!" Teena informed me. "R.J. helped. He crunched up the potato chips with a rolling pin. See, they're on the top. Eight minutes in the microwave. On high."

We didn't have a microwave, of course. It didn't matter. Tuna casserole is school cafeteria food. I wouldn't eat it anyway.

"Superman, you run back out to the car. Get the Jell-O out of the front seat."

More school cafeteria food. R.J. swooped out of the kitchen and out the front door, letting the screen slam behind him.

A couple of minutes later, he flew in with the bowl of Jell-O. He was holding it with one hand on top of his head. You could see the pirate's hat squashed underneath it. If he were my kid, I'd keep him in time-out permanently.

"Half's got fruit cocktail, half is plain," Teena explained, pointing to the Jell-O. She removed the bowl from his head and handed it to me. "I didn't know which kind y'all liked."

How about neither, I thought. I was surprised they hadn't brought pea pearls and carrot coins. We'd have the entire school lunch menu.

"Well, thanks for coming by and all." I started toward the door.

"That's what friends are for." Teena plopped down onto one of the kitchen chairs, R.J. sat on her lap, and Annabelle got busy at the counter, making coffee. Reese leaned against the door frame. They were here to stay.

"My hair color was supposed to be platinum beige," Teena remarked. She must have noticed my looking at it. "Those colors on the box never do come out right."

Her hair was amazing, big and shiny like a trophy, a pale pink one.

Annabelle must've been thinking the same thing. "Do you fix all those curls every morning?"

Each curl was a work of art, solid as if it had been preserved with floor wax.

Teena was more than happy to explain. "The way it's done is you wear a sleep bonnet to bed, and you sleep on a satin pillow. You have to do both. If you're careful, you can last nearly a week. That's one thing I learned in cosmetology college."

She must have also learned about the wonders of blue eye shadow. It stretched from her eyelashes to the bottom of her eyebrows.

"Annabelle Wynette, you ought to let your hair grow out," Teena bubbled. "I'd like to fix it for you, but I can't do nothing with those little sprigs. You could buy yourself a wiglet. I could fix it then, make it last a week like mine. And Shelby, hon, I could do yours now. It's just the right length. You want me to fix it while y'all are here?"

I said something about how we probably wouldn't have that much time, but that I appreciated the offer. Maybe I could come back to visit, sometime before Halloween. Of course, I didn't say that last bit.

"I'd like to get ahold of your mama's hair," Teena went on. "The way she's got it all pulled back is pitiful."

I couldn't believe it. She was making fun of my mother's Georgia O'Keeffe original hairdo. Reese stood at the door, grinning and chewing on a toothpick. He didn't have to worry about his hair. He kept it covered under a cowboy hat.

R.J. reached up and put his finger inside one of his mother's stiff curls. "Hi, Lois!" he said.

"Stop it!" Teena hollered. "I'm not Lois Lane!" She slapped at the air like he was a gnat. "I fell asleep on the couch the other day. R.J. stuck about fifty of those tiny cars up in my hair."

He grinned and pulled a tiny bulldozer out of his pocket. He shoved it inside one of the tunnels on his mother's head.

"Run outside," Teena scolded. "Go play. And don't jump off anything. Or into anything." He swooped out the door.

Annabelle set Ophelia down on the linoleum. "You go play too," she cooed.

"So," Teena said, sitting back in her chair. "Tell me about yourself, Shelby. Got a boyfriend?"

"Not currently." *Not ever,* I was thinking. I couldn't believe she was asking, especially with Reese standing right there.

Teena poured herself a cup of coffee. She put in four spoons of sugar and sat back down.

"Remember how I told you that Reese was in *The Tempest*, Shelby?" Annabelle asked. "He made a real cute Ferdinand. Guess who I wanted for Prospero?"

I said I didn't know.

"I tried to get Aunt Onie to play the part. I was thinking, Aunt Onie frees spirits from wood, just like Prospero. She wouldn't do it, though; said she was a wood-carver, not an actress."

Teena spoke up. "I wish y'all woulda told me that *Tempest* thang was a love story. I mighta gone. I didn't because I heard there was some kind of fairy dude in it jumping around in leotards."

"Ariel is a spirit," Annabelle explained. "He's been trapped inside a tree for years. Finally he gets freed. Wouldn't you dance around?"

Teena laughed. "Yeah, I did after two divorces. But I still say you should have put jeans and boots on him instead of tights."

"Lo-is . . . !" came a shrill voice at the back door. "I didn't mean to. . . . I'm sor . . . ry!"

"Geezy peezy!" Teena exclaimed, hopping up real fast. "He's done something!"

Annabelle stayed inside while Teena, Reese, and I headed outdoors.

Baby Superman was running in circles around the yard, his cape blowing up behind him like a circus tent.

The door to the tornado shelter had been swung open onto the grass.

"Bless my soul," Teena said as she stood at the edge of the opening and looked down. "Come look at this, Shelby."

I walked over to her, the musty smell of damp earth hitting me before I even got to the door. I walked up closer and looked down into the hole. When I saw what was there, I couldn't believe it.

I sank down on the grass, staring into the exact place my mother had stood with my father.

Chapter Thirteen

THE SKELETON OF A DRIED-UP CHRISTMAS tree stood in the cellar.

"Look! Its wings fell off!" R.J. whispered. He pointed to the carpet of needles that lay on the cement floor at the base of the tree.

"Goodnight, who woulda thought Miss Onie'd have a Christmas tree buried in the backyard? Decorated and everything." Teena stared into the hole and I did too. There was no doubt in my mind. Whoever had taken the photographs had done it down there.

I was still staring at it when Teena bent over and picked up an object on the ground. It was a lock, the sort you see on gates or storage buildings.

"R.J.!" she hollered. He was nowhere to be seen. "Superman! Get over here!" He swooped around the corner and headed toward us, his arms straight out in front of him. He peered over the edge of the hole again.

"Did you open this lock?" his mother asked.

He shrugged.

Teena lifted the door and slammed it shut. She put the lock back on and snapped it closed. "Now leave things alone."

"Mama?" came a little voice from behind us.

"Whaaat, R.J.?" Teena was out of patience.

"The kitty went down there."

"Where? Inside the cellar? Are you sure?" she said, her voice rising at the end like a balloon popping.

He nodded his head. "I didn't mean to. It was accidentally on purpose."

"Open the lock up again," Teena ordered.

He knelt on the ground and fiddled with it. "I can't," he whined. "It won't open."

She squatted down and jangled the parts up and down, then she picked up a stick and jabbed it into the keyhole. "Drat! It's not gonna open."

Superman tugged at his pants. "I have to go."

Teena sighed. "Don't tell Annabelle yet. She's gonna have a conniption fit if she finds out Ophelia's down there." She grabbed Superman's hand and headed into the house.

Far down below, under the ground, I thought I heard a tiny mew. I sat on the grass and pulled at the lock. Teena was right, it wouldn't budge. I headed back inside the house. There would have to be a key somewhere.

"Ophelia . . . Ophelia, darling . . ." Annabelle's voice echoed from the living room. I walked in. She was crawling around on the floor looking under the chairs and sofa.

"Shelby? Have you seen Ophelia anywhere?"

"No," I answered. It's true I hadn't actually *seen* her.

Superman came out of the bathroom and stood on the living room rug. The screen door slammed as his mother went back outside.

"R.J., honey, did you let Ophelia out?" Annabelle asked.

"Tell the truth," he said aloud to himself. "Okay. I did."

"Where is she?"

"In the tomato sheller."

"The tomato . . . what?"

He pointed toward the backyard. "Out there. In the tomato sheller."

"The tornado shelter!" She charged out the door.

I stayed inside, trying to think where Aunt Onie would've put the key. The rolltop desk seemed like a good place to start Underneath the cover, it was full of tiny compartments and drawers. I opened a couple; one was full of old stamps torn from letters; another was crammed full of expired coupons and old photographs that had never been put in albums.

I picked up a picture. It was Aunt Onie's backyard in the wintertime. There was snow on the ground, and white balloons were tied in all the branches of the trees and along the clothesline. It was beautiful, but sad in a way, like a celebration that had been frozen. I set it back and rolled down the desk cover. Then I ran upstairs.

I took the photograph of my parents out of my journal. When we got the cellar door open, I wanted to compare it, check out all the details. For example, I hadn't even noticed if there were shelves behind the tree. And also the ornaments. I studied the photograph. There was something silver, a bell or a mirror, hanging on the tree, near my mother's shoulder.

Outside, Annabelle was stretched out on the dirt with her ear to the cellar door. "I can't hear her!" She looked up in a panic.

Reese stood beside her. He pulled off his cowboy hat and rubbed the sides of his hair. "So Ophelia jumped into the cellar," he mused. "I thought she was afraid of the dark."

"That's Lady Macbeth. She's the one who has to have a night-light. Little Ophelia's okay in the dark, but she can't stand being alone. Ophelia . . . darling . . ." Annabelle spoke into the tin door.

Reese was about to go inside to hunt for some tools to break open the lock, when my mother and Aunt Onie drove up.

"It's Ophelia!" Annabelle cried out to them. "She's trapped in the cellar!"

My mother moved slowly, as if she were walking through deep water. Aunt Onie followed her, her hand still up in the air.

"R.J. opened the cellar," Teena explained breathlessly. She launched into the whole story. "I shut the door and locked it. I didn't know Ophelia had jumped down there. She's a nervous cat to begin with, and Annabelle's scared she might commit suicide or something." She took a long breath and the color came back into her face.

"Shelby," Aunt Onie began, "go to my bedroom. Look on the wall next to the dresser. There's a small key on a leather cord. I don't know why I keep that old lock out there. I've never used it. There's nothing valuable in the cellar."

The key was exactly where she'd said it would be. I lifted it off the nail and headed back through the house. On the way I saw Baby Superman. He was sitting in a corner with his face to the wall. His bow and arrow and pirate's hat lay next to him.

"Troublemaker," I growled.

"It's not nice to call people names," he replied.

"Now you're having to sit in the corner."

"No I'm not. It's time-out."

"Whatever. Did you know they have jails for little kids like you? They're in Patagonia. The guards are giants and they make you sit at a table by yourself and eat broccoli and spinach all day long. At night you get lima beans and brussels sprouts. And when you go to bed, you don't get a drink of water or a story."

"You're not supposed to talk to me. Nobody is."

I squatted down. "Did you really put Ophelia down in that cellar?"

"She went by himself."

"Herself," I corrected. "Your grammar is atrocious."

"She is not! She made me a George."

"What?"

"A George monkey. Gramma sewed it out of socks. It's a curiwas George."

"Oh, Curious George. Remember the story about how he swallowed the puzzle piece?"

"And went to the hospital. And the doctor got it out."

"Smart kid!" Without thinking, I reached down and gave his shoulders a little hug. "How much time did you get?"

"To when the buzzer goes off." He looked up at me.

He reminded me of myself when I was little. No brothers, no sisters. Like me, he probably didn't even know his father. All he had was a pink-haired mother with a string of idiot boyfriends. At least he had a grandmother who'd make him a sock monkey.

I reached out my hand to him. "You come with me. Don't run off, either, or I'll sell you for a nickel to those Patagonians."

"You're teasing me!"

"Come on. Let's go tell your mother I'll keep an eye on you. Somebody needs to. You're a mess."

He put his hand in mine. It was sticky. I looked down at him. He sure was an ugly little kid.

"First, we're going to take this key outside and get Ophelia. What a stupid name for a cat! Don't you think so?"

"I fink it's stooopid!"

I squatted down again and looked him in the eyes. "Put your tongue against your top teeth." I showed him. "Now blow. Th . . . ," I said. "Say 'th . . . ink.' "

He tried it. "Think!" He grinned. There was something red and sticky around his lips.

"Now say, 'I *think* it's stupid.' "

"I think it's *stupid*!" he shouted.

"Good!"

He grinned up at me.

"Did you get into the red Jell-O?"

"Tell the truth!" he said.

"I hope you ate it all, especially the fruit cocktail side."

"I ate it all a little bit," he admitted.

"Good. Now, come on, let's go outside. We have to let Ophelia out of the cellar before she scares herself to death."

Outside, the lock opened easily, and we swung the door open.

"Ophelia . . . O . . . phel . . . ia . . ." Annabelle called down into the hole. She said the name like it was covered in flowers, twirling the *l*'s like an opera singer. "O . . . phe . . . *llll* . . . ia."

No cat appeared. "The last time I went down into one of those things I had a panic attack. I'm just a tiny bit claustrophobic," Annabelle said.

My mother sat at the edge of the hole. She had her knees drawn up under her chin, her arms wrapped around her legs. She hates tornado shelters too. She'd as soon be blown away by a cyclone as go down into a cellar. I couldn't figure out why she'd ever get her picture taken down there.

"I'll go," I volunteered. The photograph was in my pocket. I wanted to compare.

I started down the concrete steps, practically forgetting about Ophelia. When I got to the bottom, I pulled the light cord, but the light had burned out. Still, I could see well enough. A ray of sunlight slanted through the hole onto the tree. I pulled the photograph out of my pocket.

The shelves were there, only most of them were empty. Two or three jars were still full of tomatoes or green beans floating in cloudy liquid.

What in the world was a Christmas tree doing in a storm shelter? It didn't make sense. I could tell from the ornaments that it was the same tree. The silver mirror decorated in glitter hung in the exact same spot that it did in the photograph. I stood there staring at it, memorizing the details.

Suddenly, in the shadows of the dark cellar, I began to see my mother. She stood in front of the tree, her hands across her stomach, holding me inside. Then I saw him. He stood next to her; and for an instant, right when I was about to see his face, the sunlight caught the edge of the mirror and I glanced down. It was his silver belt buckle I saw, not his face.

I shut my eyes. I didn't want to see it anymore. When I looked up again, he had disappeared. The whole image was gone and I was shaking all over. I put the photograph inside my pocket.

The cat. Suddenly I remembered her. I knelt on the floor and called her.

"Ophelia . . ." No sound. "Ophelia . . ." For some reason my voice came out quivery, like I'd been scared to death. My stomach felt queasy.

There was a cot next to the wall opposite the tree. It was covered with an army blanket that hung crookedly to the floor. I crawled over to it and pulled up the edge of the blanket. No kitty. Nothing but cobwebs.

I was about to stand up when I saw it. It was just a small matchbox, but it was covered in rubber bands, and something about it made me curious. I checked for spiders, then reached under the cot and pulled it out.

I shook it. It made a soft shuffling sound. Something else was hidden in the box, not matches. I slowly pulled off a couple of the rubber bands.

"Shelby!" It was Annabelle. "Shelby! Come on up! Hurry!"

I shoved the matchbox into my pocket next to the photograph and headed back up the stairs. I stepped onto the grass next to my mother.

"Excuse me, sir!" Baby Superman was tugging on the back of my shirt. He pointed to the sky. "I fink, I mean I *th*ink that O-*pee*-a is in the tree."

I looked up. A white ball sat high up on one of the branches of a pine tree. She wasn't moving at all. Even Annabelle couldn't coax her down.

Reese went to the shed for a ladder, and when he returned Annabelle started climbing up. I couldn't understand what she was saying, but she was talking in a high voice to Ophelia, trying to convince her she'd be all right. Finally, she leaned over and reached for her.

She inched down the ladder holding Ophelia around the chest, the cat's legs dangling under the grip of her arms.

When they got to the bottom, Ophelia leaped to the ground. She rolled onto her back playfully like nothing had happened. To me, if anybody needed a time-out, she did.

Aunt Onie had gone inside, but my mother sat on the grass next to the open cellar. She was staring down into the hole like it was a grave.

Pretty soon she got up and wandered back up to the house. She entered her room again without saying a word to anyone.

Chapter Fourteen

"OPHELIA'S RIDING UP FRONT," ANNABELLE announced. The cat's narrow white head poked over the dash like a hood ornament. Since she hadn't died or anything, she was getting treated like a princess. Annabelle stroked her neck and popped kitty treats into her mouth every time she mewed.

It was supposed to be early when we left for the canyon, but it was past lunch already. We'd had Teena's tuna casserole and peanut butter and jelly sandwiches. My mother hadn't come out of her bedroom since we'd gotten Ophelia out of the tree, and Aunt Onie had settled in for a long nap. For me, it was either stay at the house and be bored to death or go to the canyon with Reese. I'd decided to go.

Annabelle said it would take almost an hour to drive there, so I settled back for a long ride. According to my mother, after Georgia O'Keeffe traipsed around in the canyon, she switched from using plain black and white to using color. I didn't expect anything that dramatic to happen. I just wanted a change of scenery, a rest from all the worries that were on my mind. When Reese and I climbed into the backseat and we pulled out onto the road, I leaned back and shut my eyes.

Around that time, Annabelle started droning on and on, about her plays, her cats, and anything else she could think of.

"Shelby, would you like to take a kitten home with you? I have a new one." She peered through the rearview mirror at me.

I said my mother wouldn't let me. She doesn't believe in pets. They die too much.

"People." Annabelle stated flatly. "They don't get their pets spayed, first of all. Then they dump the babies out in the country. Every so often, I save one. Like this one. His name is Hamlet."

"It sounds like he'd fit in with the rest," Reese commented, the first thing he'd said the whole way.

"Except he's a boy. He's real cute, though," Annabelle urged. "Ophelia's wild about him. But I told her we can't keep him. Think about it, Shelby, okay?"

I said I would. It really didn't matter what my mother said anymore. I was going to live with Roo. Still, I couldn't expect to move in with all my stuff and a cat too.

We drove on and on for at least fifty miles, passing through the most boring and flat land in the world. I was beginning to doubt the canyon even existed. Then Annabelle pulled off the road.

She opened the front door of the van and stepped out. I saw her looking up into the sky, which had filled with clouds since we left Aunt Onie's. Then she stuck her head back in.

"This weather is starting to look strange," she said. "I wonder if we ought to turn around." The blue sky had turned a light green, like mashed-up lima beans.

Reese thought we should go on. The weather in this part of Texas is totally unpredictable. There'd been a lot of rain lately and tornado watches, but nothing bad had happened.

"This might be Shelby's only chance to see the canyon," he argued. I didn't care if I missed the canyon or not; it wasn't like seeing Halley's comet or anything. The canyon would be waiting forever.

Annabelle pulled back onto the road. After a while the sun peeked out and everything looked okay again.

Reese slid his hat over his eyes, stuck a toothpick in his mouth, and leaned back against the seat.

"When the air gets so still, almost solid, something usually happens," Annabelle remarked into her rearview mirror. "It's the calm before the storm."

The air did feel heavy and quiet, but I wasn't that worried. It'd be unlikely that a tornado would dip down into a deep canyon. It would probably just skim over the top.

Except for Ophelia mewing for more cookies, it was quiet for several more miles. Then Annabelle got all excited. "There it is!" she exclaimed.

Reese sat up and put his hat back on. In the distance I could see a gigantic chasm. It was like the entire earth had split open.

As we got closer, everything brown turned red; giant red rocks and cliffs streaked with yellow plunged into a canyon, eight hundred feet deep in places, according to Annabelle. She wound the van slowly inside, and the road curved as if we were traveling on the rim of a huge, deep cup. As we circled, we descended deeper and deeper into the hole.

Annabelle rolled down her window and poked her head out. "See how quiet it is?"

It was quiet. It was as if a whole world had stopped in the middle of a monumental explosion, and we'd happened onto it.

Annabelle talked like a tour guide as she pointed out rock formations and various colors etched into the sandstone. There were the Spanish Skirts, which really did look like huge skirts ruffled in red and yellow; and there was the Devil's Slide, where a lot of people had broken their arms, legs, and necks; and there was the Sad Monkey and the Lighthouse. Even Reese had his favorite, the Sleeping Indian.

I couldn't see what he was talking about at first because the Indian was part of a larger rock jutting into the sky. Then I saw his nose, followed by his mouth and chin. He lay on his back, his stone face staring into the clouds.

Reese knew the history. "When the Kiowa were driven out, one Indian refused to go," he said. "Or at least that's what I believed when I was a kid. I thought the guy turned into rock rather than move again."

I understood completely. I'd been through the moves. Now my life was even more complicated. I couldn't get the truth about my father. And my mother didn't even care. If I could turn into a rock, I would.

"You okay?" Reese asked.

I looked down, feeling as if I were balancing on the thin edge of the canyon all by myself.

My hands were trembling.

"Shelby?"

"Sure. I'm fine," I said. I gazed out the window, squeezing my palms together.

"Look, Shelby! Over there's Lighthouse Peak." Annabelle pointed to a rock formation in the distance. If I'd gone to the beach with Roo, I'd be looking at a real lighthouse.

Finally, we got to the stables.

"Meet me back here at seven," Annabelle said. "Watch the weather! There's a few caves around. Hide in one of those if it gets too bad."

We said goodbye, and she and Ophelia drove off.

Mike, the cowboy at the stables, said about a thousand acres had been fenced in for riding. "You can follow the trail and not get lost, or you can go wherever you want. There's a couple of side canyons I'd avoid, though."

I asked him about the caves Annabelle had mentioned.

"There's a few, mostly just washups," he said. "Don't go in them. Never know when one might come down on you."

"What about snakes?" I asked.

"We've got some diamondbacks. They don't usually get out in the heat, though. Now, what kind of riders are you two?"

Reese spoke up. "I can ride anything you've got. What about you, Shelby?"

"Me too. I can ride anything." I bit my bottom lip.

"You wearing those?" Mike pointed at my sneakers. "You oughta have something with a heel."

"Oh," I said. "I guess I left my boots at home."

Mike frowned and went inside the barn. When he came out again, he had two horses.

"Here's a ranch horse and a young mare," he told Reese.

"Can you manage her?" Reese asked me, nodding at the mare.

"Can she manage me? That's the question!"

I tried to copy the way Reese got on his horse, putting my left leg in the stirrup, then grabbing hold of the saddle horn with both hands and pulling myself up. Mike handed me the reins with a look that said he knew I hadn't been on too many horses.

"Just follow the trail," he suggested. We started off, Reese ahead, me following at a walk.

It wasn't as easy as I thought it would be. The horse stopped whenever she pleased, and she resisted every time I tugged at her reins. Reese looked back every so often, but I motioned him on. I wanted him to think I was doing fine.

At the first fork, my horse turned while Reese's went straight ahead. I tried to stop her, but she wouldn't pay attention. She threw her nose into the air and pulled on the reins. Then, suddenly, she plowed straight ahead. I held on.

We'd gone a ways up the trail, half a football field probably, when the wind picked up, making the leaves and branches rustle louder and louder. A limb blew across the trail in front of us and a batch of birds flew up noisily over our heads. The mare jumped nervously, and I struggled to hold the reins. Then the rain started. First it was one raindrop as big as a quarter that splattered my arm. Then it was another and another. In seconds, the rain gushed down in sheets.

It was getting hard to see, and the reins were wet and slick; the mare was going too fast, and I was scared I couldn't hold on. Then, suddenly, she stopped. I saw my chance and swung my leg over and hit the ground. As soon as I did, she started suddenly, jerked the reins out of my hands, and ran off.

I looked around in the rain, searching for Reese. He was nowhere in sight. There was a dark opening up on the side of a hill about a hundred yards from me. It was almost hidden by grass and rocks, but it looked big enough to get inside.

Then the hail started, huge chunks as big as golf balls crashing through the trees. Before I could think what to do, one smashed into me, just above my eyebrow. Covering my head with my hands, I ran as fast as I could toward the cave.

Inside, it was cool and damp. I shivered as I sat listening to the hail pound the ground above me. Surely, I thought, by now Reese would have realized I was gone.

Almost as soon as it started, the storm died down. I peeked out the opening at a clearing sky. That's when I saw Reese. He was on his horse a few feet below. I waved and he started up toward me.

"Did you know your head's bleeding?" he said when he got closer.

I reached up to touch my face above my eyebrow where it stung a little.

Reese tied his horse to a cedar bush growing out of the side of the rock and climbed up to the cave opening.

"You okay?" he asked.

My clothes were dripping wet. My horse was probably a hundred miles away by now. I was bleeding. "I'm fine," I answered.

"Let's see that cut." He held my chin with one hand and touched my eyebrow lightly with the other. It was embarrassing having him look at me that close.

"You've got a small cut over your eyebrow. Head wounds always bleed a lot. It's not bad." He reached into his back pocket and pulled out a bandanna.

"Hold still." He put one hand firmly on my shoulder. "Close your eyes."

I held my breath as soon as he touched me.

He dabbed the blood from above my eyebrow and I felt him examining the cut. "It's just a scratch. You sure you're okay?"

"I'm fine," I said. "By the way, how much do horses cost? I lost mine."

"She's not lost. She'll go right back to the stables."

"Are you sure?"

"I know horses."

"I guess this means I won't win Horsewoman of the Year, right?'

"Probably not." He grinned.

"I'd never been on a horse before," I confessed.

"No kidding," he said, giving my sleeve a little tug. He sat down in the opening beside me. "Ever explored a cave?"

"Well, I've seen a little bit of this one." I looked behind me. There wasn't much to see. The whole thing was smaller than my closet at home.

"Come on," he said, crawling past me into the larger space, which wasn't big enough to stand up in but was plenty big enough to sit in.

"What if it falls in on us?" I looked up at the ceiling, where a small hole let in a shaft of light.

"I've been in these things all my life," he said, looking back at me.

He took off his hat to keep it from scraping the ceiling, leaned against the wall, and motioned for me to come on. I crawled on my hands and knees toward him. The cave smelled a little like Aunt Onie's tornado shelter, like wet dirt mixed with something old.

The walls were slick and grayish brown, and the light was even grayer, like a huge shadow had settled on top of us. I squirmed around, trying to get more comfortable, and as I did, I felt the matchbox. It was still in my pocket along with the photograph. I reached inside and pulled them out.

"What's that?" Reese asked as I laid the photograph on the rock beside me. It was damp, but not ruined.

"The picture is of my parents, minus my father's face, that is." I held up the matchbox. "The box, it's just something I found in Aunt Onie's tornado shelter. It was under the cot."

I handed it to him, and he shook it. "Sounds like a jigsaw puzzle. A tiny one," he joked. "Here. Open it."

I took the box from him and peeled off one of the rubber bands, pretending to shoot it at him. It broke in half even before I'd aimed well. The box must have been down in the cellar a long time. I pulled off a couple more of the bands, then the rest.

"Wait," Reese said, digging inside his pocket. He pulled out a small penlight hooked to a key chain. "It's too dark in here to see anything." He flicked the light on and shined a tiny red circle of light on the cave wall.

"Okay, ready?" he asked. It was the grand opening.

I laughed and slid open the box.

And then I froze.

A pile of faces stared up at me. I poured them into my hand, pressing hard against my knee to stop the shaking.

"Who is it?" Reese asked, shining his light on the tiny faces my mother had cut from the photographs.

I stared at one of the cutouts, the curly blond hair, the eyes, the mouth, and suddenly I knew him.

The memory opened like a huge sore, and I saw every part of it. I was maybe three years old. My father stood over me, shouting. I saw his angry red face and his shiny silver belt buckle, how it came at me, lashing out like a snake, over and over, biting into my skin. And the worst part. I saw myself. Me standing in the bathtub. Naked, dripping wet. Crying, sharp scared cries like an animal and the pink bathwater on my toes and my mother's skirt at the door, the back of her skirt, turning away from me, running away.

The memory chased me out of the cave.

There was nowhere to run. Everywhere around me were rocks, giant and looming like big red faces, and the Spanish Skirts swept around me, but I couldn't hide under them. I collapsed to the ground, shielding my head with my hands, vomiting into the dirt.

Reese was bending over me. I felt his flannel shirt against me.

"Shelby? What's wrong? Whatever it is, it's okay," he said. "You're all right." I felt him rocking me, holding me tight.

He had a canteen of water and he helped me clean myself up. Then he guided me to his horse.

"You'll have to get on behind me," he said after he'd gotten on. I stood there shivering, still wet from the rain all the way to my underwear.

He reached out his hand and told me to put my foot in the stirrup. I did what he said, grabbing the saddle with my other hand and straining to pull myself up behind him.

"Hold on," he instructed.

I put my hands on the ridge at the back of the saddle.

"Not like that, Shelby. Put your arms around my waist."

Slowly, I put my arms around him. His body was hard and damp, and I could feel his heart beating on the insides of my elbows all the way to the top of Lighthouse Peak.

There the canyon opened up all around us into beautiful deep fans of color. "I wanted you to see something really pretty," Reese said quietly.

We looked out over the rim of the canyon. It seemed as though we were standing on a rocky beach, the sky stretching into a bright blue ocean. Then the image of my mother floated like a dead fish to the top of my mind. Somewhere between my father's red face and the shiny belt buckle, I saw her, the back of her dress, leaving me all alone.

Chapter Fifteen

"WANT TO TASTE A PRICKLY PEAR?" REESE said, sliding off his horse at the base of the lighthouse. He took out his pocketknife and cut a red bulb from a cactus, sliced it in half and gave me some.

"Suck it," he said. "Like this." He put it between his teeth. I followed the motion, feeling numb. The pear was warm, sweet against the bitter taste in my mouth, and its sweetness lingered as we made our way down the rocks.

My horse had been back at the stables a good while. Just like Reese said, she'd gone straight back. Mike was glad to see us. He said he'd worried and had planned to get someone to look for us if we didn't get back soon. Reese turned his horse in and we sat outside the barn and drank root beers.

I didn't mention what had happened at the cave, and Reese didn't either. Maybe if I didn't think about it, it would go away, disappear like a bad dream.

We left the stables for the Sad Monkey Railroad. Reese said it looked like a child's ride, but he assured me adults rode it too. The train had small metal seats and an open top, like a ride at a carnival, but it took you through the canyon so that you could see everything close up. I sank into the seat and closed my eyes. I felt weak and sore, and tired of seeing red, red rocks and red cliffs, the red muddy ground. His face had been red, too, and the water. It was red.

I heard a voice. It was Reese. He was talking about an Indian skeleton he and his dad had found in the back of a cave. When they left it and went back later, it was gone.

"My father was an archaeologist," I said. It was after he'd been an astronaut, in the sixth grade after we'd read about King Tut's tomb.

"You kidding? We could have used him. We never did find those bones again. Went through about a dozen caves, searching."

"He wasn't really."

"What?"

"An archaeologist. He wasn't one. I was just joking." I'd been the one looking for bones. They were here all the time, inside me.

The train chugged alongside rocks and mesquite trees, cedars and yucca, the conductor speaking into his microphone, pointing everything out. "You'll still find some arrowheads and buffalo bones out here," he said.

"Maybe that's what you found," I told Reese. "Buffalo bones."

"What would a buffalo be doing in a cave?"

I shrugged. "I've seen stranger things. A Christmas tree in a tornado shelter, for example."

"That was weird," he agreed.

My father's face loomed over me again. The memory was too new. It kept showing itself to me. I shook my head.

At the same time, the train eased to a stop at the depot, a combination Sno-Kone stand and ticket office. Reese jumped off. He paid for two blue Sno-Kones and handed me one.

"Let's walk the road back toward the stables," he suggested. "If we walk along the edge, we might see the van." It was okay with me. I could walk off the side of a cliff and it would be okay.

"You're quiet, Shelby." I could tell Reese was still wondering about what had happened earlier, but it was too fresh. I couldn't talk about it yet.

I kicked at some pebbles and didn't answer.

"What happened down at the cave? What scared you so bad?"

I shook my head, sucking on the blue ice.

Finally, he patted me on the back awkwardly and we walked on.

A few minutes later, after we'd finished our Sno-Kones, Annabelle's van passed us. Reese hollered and waved and she slowed down and backed up.

"You two look worn out!" she said, sticking her face out the window. "Get in!"

I looked up. The van was full: Teena, Aunt Onie, Baby Superman, and a cat, plus Annabelle, of course. Then there was my mother.

A large orange cat sat in the front with Annabelle. The cat wore a jeweled collar. She had a rhinestone stud in the top of each ear, and she hissed at Reese and me as we climbed into the front seat next to her.

"Meet Lady Macbeth!" Annabelle said, pushing a treat into the cat's mouth.

"Shelby, you look like you've seen a ghost. Your lips are blue! You okay?"

I muttered that I was fine. Annabelle started down the road again.

"Hey, Shelf-by, we brought a pic-a-nic," R.J. sang out. He was still wearing his Superman costume. The kid needed therapy.

"It was Teena's idea to have a picnic," Annabelle filled in.

My mother sat staring out the window, her dark hair pulled back into a bun at the back of her head. We passed three creek crossings with picnic signs. Finally, on the fourth, we pulled into a grassy area.

My mother climbed out and guided Aunt Onie to the table. Her sore hand rested now in a sling made out of a head scarf.

"You don't think Lady Mac will run off?" Reese asked when Annabelle set the cat on the ground.

"No, she won't even try to leave," Annabelle said, rubbing her behind the ears. "I bribed her. She'll do anything for a kitty cookie." Lady Macbeth arched her back and rubbed against Annabelle's leg.

Teena giggled as she pulled apart some wire coat hangers, stretching them into roasting spears. "What you need, Annabelle Wynette, is some boy cats. Then the girls'd mind their manners."

Annabelle shook her head, smiling. "Not these girls. They could care less about boys. They've all been fixed. Lady Macbeth would as soon kill a male as get close to one."

Aunt Onie chuckled at the joke, but my mother didn't.

"I wish I could climb up on one of those cliffs again," Aunt Onie said, looking at the canyon around us. "Seems like the older I get, the lower down I get."

"I know what you mean," Teena agreed. "That's why I got me a Wonder Bra." She giggled and I was pretty sure she was about to unbutton her shirt and show us, but Superman swooped past us to the creek and she had to take off and catch him.

Reese pretended not to listen. He was a few feet away, working on getting a fire started.

"The last time I came out here was with you, Zoe, you and—" Aunt Onie stopped herself. "The moon that night got as big as a tractor tire. Orange. Lordy, I never seen orange like that since. Do you remember, honey?"

"I paid a dollar twenty-nine a pound for oranges last week," my mother responded. Her words came out stiff and lifeless.

"It was like God punched a great big hole in the sky and heaven shined through as big as life. Never thought it'd be orange, though," Aunt Onie mused.

"I'd be mad." Teena jabbed a wiener onto her coat hanger. "Lots of people would be mad, expecting golden streets and all, then it turns up orange! Probably be some lawsuits over that one."

Aunt Onie chuckled. "What if heaven was completely orange, the streets, the harps, the angels, even God!"

"Well, I hope I never see it, then!" Teena ended the conversation.

"Where's R.J.?" I asked. Teena had returned without him.

"He's on the other side of the van, planting another one of those seeds. Cantaloupe this time."

I walked over to him and squatted down in the dirt.

"Why are you planting all these seeds?"

"For a sister," he said. "It might be you."

"Sorry, I don't get it."

"I told Mama I wanted a sister. She said the boy has to plant the seed." He patted a little mound of dirt with the palm of his hand. "Now we have to get some water. Else it won't work."

"How about if I agree to be your big sister? You don't even have to plant all those seeds."

"For real? You'll come live at my house?"

"No, I can't do that. I have to go back to my school."

"Will you write me a letter?"

I said I would, and we walked back to the picnic table. Mechanically, my mother was spreading a paper cloth on the table. She was a million miles away.

"You must've got baptized in the creek, Shelby," Aunt Onie remarked.

"She nearly did," Reese answered, grinning at me.

"You need some waterproof mascara," Teena offered. "Come over to the store. We've got your waterproof foundation, waterproof eye shadow, and waterproof lipstick; also eyeliner and blush, all waterproof."

"Why don't you just put a skin diver's mask on her and be done with it?" Annabelle joked.

My mother got up and sat down next to the fire. She pulled her knees up to her chin and wrapped her arms around them like she always does.

"Hot dog, Zoe?" Annabelle asked.

She shook her head. "No thanks. I'm not really hungry."

"Come on, Zoe. How about a nice big weenie?" Teena grinned, jiggling the frankfurter on the end of the wire. My mother didn't even smile.

"Maybe I'll roast a marshmallow. Later. I don't want anything right now."

"Got man troubles?" Teena inquired as she poked her wiener into the fire.

"What?" my mother answered foggily.

"Do you have a boyfriend back home?"

"Um? Not anymore. I did, though."

"Was he cute?"

"He frowned a lot."

"What was his profession?" Teena wouldn't let up.

"Well"—she cleared her throat—"he worked at an auto parts store. He liked fixing carburetors and fuel pumps. He liked women he could fix, too."

"I could use a tune-up myself," Teena joked. She slid her blackened wiener off the hanger into a hot dog bun and squirted mustard all over the top.

It was true about John D. He did like his way about things. But at least he hadn't hurt anyone.

Lady Macbeth padded up next to me, rubbing against my leg. I reached down and petted her. Then she let me hold her in my lap and stroke her back.

"You should feel privileged, Shelby," Annabelle said, looking up at me. "Lady M. doesn't trust many people."

"Me either," I said, looking right at my mother.

Just before the sun disappeared behind the Sleeping Indian, the sky turned bright orange. By then Aunt Onie needed her pain medicine, Superman was whining, and Lady Macbeth came out from under a pile of wood with a feather in her mouth. Nothing felt like heaven.

Aunt Onie got in the front seat with Annabelle this time so that she could use one of the armrests. Lady Macbeth and my mother got in behind them, next to Teena and Baby Superman. Reese and I climbed in the back, the third row of seats, which faced backward.

It was almost dark by the time we came up out of the park. The canyon faded to a shadow on the ground; then it was gone. The wind pounded at the windows like it wanted in, but Annabelle didn't even slow down. After a while, after the night got completely dark, Reese reached over and took my hand. It was okay with me.

According to my mother, cattle used to escape from the wind by traveling down the canyon's trails into the deep parts. She learned this from Georgia O'Keeffe, who had said the cows looked like black lace along the canyon rim, and when they went down inside, their bellows echoed like a strange kind of music. To Georgia O'Keeffe the canyon was both beautiful and scary.

As we rode away from it, after all that had happened, I knew exactly what she meant.

Chapter Sixteen

T<small>HE NEXT MORNING THE SUN FROM THE ATTIC</small> window awakened me. First it made a square near the foot of the bed; then, as usual, it crawled across the quilt and settled on my face. I sat up. When I did, I felt sad all over. There wasn't even a line in my journal to describe it.

A mother is supposed to protect her children. She's not supposed to leave them under a bridge or in a park or standing naked in a bathtub.

The photograph of my mother and father standing in front of the Christmas tree lay on the bedside table, the pile of cutout heads next to it. I reached across the bed and picked up one of my father's faces and placed it inside the hole in the photograph. He was a little lopsided, but he was smiling, gazing down at my mother's stomach, where I was probably sleeping.

My parents looked happy, like friendly paper dolls. In the light my father didn't look one bit scary. He seemed nice. I wondered what had happened to change all that.

What had caused his rage? What had caused my mother to just stand there and do nothing?

I felt miserable. Finally I pulled myself out of bed and dressed, slowly forcing my legs into my jeans, my arms into the sleeves of my shirt. Then I gathered up the faces, one at a time, and dropped them into the pocket of my jeans. Slowly I went down the stairs, taking each step as if I were descending into deep water.

Aunt Onie sat alone at the kitchen table. She had removed her bandage and had propped her sore hand in front of her. The cut stretched across her palm like a pink centipede with black legs. It was puffy and still oozed blood in places, especially in the deepest part between her thumb and forefinger.

"Are you okay?" I asked, looking around for my mother.

"I'm fine, honey. Your mama, she carried herself to town. Said she had some phone calls to make. She'll be back directly."

"Did she say who she was calling?"

"Rosie something or other."

"That's her boss at Roses and Wreaths." I wondered what she was really doing.

Aunt Onie nodded toward a dinner plate stacked with big square packages of gauze. "I was fixing to doctor up this old hand of mine."

"I'll do it." I reached for the bottle of hydrogen peroxide. "Come stand over the sink."

Some things are easy. You don't even have to think. Pour the cleanser over the stitches. Pat dry. Squeeze antibiotic ointment onto a cotton swab. Gently trace along the cut, even though it jags in and out as if it can't decide which way to go. Lay a clean square of gauze across the palm and tape it around the edges, stretching the tape across the top of the hand.

"Done!" I said. "It's a good thing you didn't sever a tendon, Aunt Onie."

"I won't be carving no more."

"Probably not," I agreed.

"People used to say it was plain magic the way I could pull a bird out of a piece of mesquite."

"You made them for a lot of children."

She nodded.

"What about you, Shelby?"

I looked up startled. "What do you mean?"

"I mean you got a power in you. You're a healer."

"I learned first aid in health class. Everybody has to take it."

"Not just my hand, honey."

Aunt Onie wasn't making sense again. And she didn't know me at all. She didn't know I'm an *At Risk*. She didn't know anything. She was a crazy old lady who wore knee-high hose with Bermuda shorts and red plastic rain bonnets when it wasn't even raining.

After I got her settled on the couch and opened the curtains, I went back up to my room in the attic. I sat on the edge of the bed, slowly turning through the pages of my journal. I stopped at part of Ms. P.'s favorite poem: "Spring and Fall," by Gerard Manley Hopkins. I'd only recorded the beginning, but the lines echoed from the page like long sad notes on a violin.

Margaret, are you grieving
Over Goldengrove unleaving?

It wasn't just about trees losing their leaves. I could see that now. It was about my father, and about me. Maybe Roo was right. Maybe I had hoped he lived in a golden castle somewhere. Maybe I had hoped that if I really needed him, he'd find me.

After a while I crawled into bed with my clothes on and went to sleep. It was the safest place. I didn't want to think anymore.

By lunch, my mother still hadn't gotten back. I'd had to fry Aunt Onie's bologna, make it into a sandwich with sliced okra pickles, get her snuff out of its hiding place, bring her a Dr Pepper, and wrap her up in the yellow-and-orange afghan. She looked like something in a cocoon.

It was late afternoon when my mother finally got in, and she didn't even apologize. She came right into the living room, kicked off her shoes, and stepped barefoot onto the coffee table. It was just like we were at home.

"I have an announcement!" she said.

Aunt Onie stirred inside her cocoon, barely even listening.

My mother looked straight at me. "Shelby, you're not going to like this. Not at first."

I hate it when my mother talks like that.

"It's about New Mexico."

She paused.

"Here at Aunt Onie's, we're only three or four hours away, and . . ."

She took a deep breath. "The bottom line is this. I made some calls, the movers, Roses and Wreaths, your school. It's set. We're moving."

I sprang up from the sofa.

"Listen," she said, reaching out for me. "About your snooping around in my room, finding those pictures. I'm okay with it now."

"Well, I'm not!" I jerked away from her.

"Shelby, please . . . when we get to New Mexico, it'll be a new start."

I did it before I even stopped to think, all in one motion, reaching into my pocket and flinging them at her. The faces fell like snow all around her hair and onto the floor.

For a moment no one said a word; then I heard myself. I was screaming.

"How could you let him hurt me? How could you?"

She looked at me, stunned.

"Shelby . . ."

Suddenly I was outside, running, past the tornado shelter, past the pine trees, the windmill, the stock tank, the barn, into the empty field. I ran until Aunt Onie's house became a dot; then I ran some more until I was in the middle of nowhere and the ground reached up and pulled me down.

I lay there out of breath. I even thought about dying. I thought about how some kids might find my bones, half buried and partly bleached by the sun. Maybe they would think they had found the bones of one of Aunt Onie's angels, who had blown off the roof during a dust storm.

People at the museum, of course, would prove them wrong. They'd say, "These are just the bones of a young girl who lost herself in the middle of a wheat field. That's all."

Roo says crying is good. She says tears are like oil. They keep the heart from drying up and totally breaking apart. I disagree. When Ishmael was in the middle of the ocean all by himself, did he cry? I say no. He was already floating in salt water. What good would it have done?

After a while, a long time it seemed, I felt her coming. Like a shadow that falls on you before you see the source of it, I knew she was there. I saw her blood-splattered sneakers and the hem of her flowered dress.

"What are you doing out here?" It was me asking.

"Honey, I've been circling the land for years, looking for lost children."

"I'm not lost."

"Your mama is."

"It's her own fault."

"She's hanging on to the bed, crying out her soul, honey."

"She let him hurt me."

"He was so big, Shelby. She was always so tiny."

"What about me? I wasn't big." My voice sounded like a little girl's. I was three years old again.

"I know it, honey."

Aunt Onie knelt down beside me, her eyes sorrowful.

"After he hit you, your mama waited till the middle of the night, then she wrapped you in a blanket and sneaked out, barefoot so's not to make any noise. She left everything she owned."

I looked into the sky. A thousand clouds hung over me in big swollen lumps. I watched them bump into each other, the big ones swallowing the little ones.

"Why did he hate me so much?" It was the little girl's voice again.

Aunt Onie put her thin arms around my shoulders. I felt her sore hand press against my back.

"He hated himself, not you. Every place he looked, he saw himself, and he wanted to hurt what he saw."

"But they were happy before I was born." I was thinking about the photograph, how they were smiling.

She shook her head. "No, honey. He'd hurt her lots of times. She'd leave and come back, and he'd promise to be different. That's what the tree was about."

"What do you mean?"

Aunt Onie brought her sore hand from around my back and touched the buttons on the front of her dress.

"First, I have to explain something about your mama. When she was a little girl, she got all mixed up about love. She'd been shut in a storm shelter for punishment of some sort. They took the light out of the socket, closed her up for hours in the dark. It terrified her. She never told anybody except me and . . ."

She stopped and swallowed, as if she were having trouble getting the word to come out.

"Rowdy. That was his name, honey."

The name stirred inside of me like a bad dream.

"Your mama left when she found out she was pregnant, said she wasn't ever coming back on account of how he'd treated her. But he begged her to let him come get her, promised her he'd changed. She didn't want him to know where she was, said she'd come on her own if she decided to. That's when she came in on the bus. He could be real charming, you know."

"It was snowing the night the sheriff brought her out here," I said, remembering what she'd told me earlier.

"Yes. The next day, we looked out back and the whole yard was covered in snow, and Rowdy had decorated everything in white balloons, had them hanging from the pine branches, the clothesline, everywhere. That's when he hauled the Christmas tree down to the tornado shelter."

I still didn't get it. "Why there?"

"Honey, he wanted your mama to believe he'd really changed. I 'spect he wanted to believe it too. He convinced her to go down in the storm shelter. Said he wanted to show her that she didn't have to be afraid anymore. Everything was all pretty and lit up."

"She fell down the cellar steps," I added, feeling the bitterness in my mouth. I knew that wasn't what had really happened.

Aunt Onie looked at me with her sad eyes.

"She must've thrown those faces down into the cellar before she left," I said.

Part of a smile crept across Aunt Onie's face. "Your mama. She always was dramatic."

I agreed, but I wanted her to go on. "What happened next?"

"She left again, had you, lived alone for a good while, but he finally found her. You must have been about three when he moved back to Red Valley. He was alone when he came by the house. Wanted me to tell him where your mama was. I said I didn't know."

"Did you know where we were?"

"No, she didn't even tell me. I'd gotten one note from her, saying he hurt you and that she'd never see me again because she could never come back, not to Red Valley."

"What happened to him, to Rowdy?"

"Later, I caught him out back with the door to the shelter open. I told him to leave, and he did. Maybe he was just going to carry the tree up, I don't know, but I didn't give him a chance to explain. I just shut up the cellar and never went down there again."

"Did he move away from Red Valley?"

She shook her head. "He stayed here, off and on, at the Driftwood Star Motel."

"He's here? In Red Valley?"

"Not anymore, honey. Last week, he ran his truck into a lake between here and Oklahoma City. He lived a reckless life. It was just a matter of time."

So it was over. For years my mother had read the obituaries from Red Valley. We had come here because she had to make sure.

Aunt Onie reached out with her good hand and helped me up. She didn't need the evening star to get home. Her thin cotton dress swung loosely from her shoulders as she made her way through the grass, sure and certain. She knew the way, and I followed her.

It was dusk by the time we saw the house. When the heat of the day melts down, things get hazy. My mother calls it Texas fog. In the distance Aunt Onie's house looked like something that had been underwater for a long time, then had washed up on the land to dry.

When we got up closer, I saw a faded green pickup truck parked out by the gate. Reese was waiting out on the porch. He had on shorts, a T-shirt, sneakers, and a baseball cap, like a regular guy.

He grinned and I sat down next to him.

"Where's your horse?" I asked.

He pointed to the truck.

"You can drive?"

"Been driving tractors all my life."

I was thinking. What if memories are like pieces of a jigsaw puzzle? What if they line up inside you, waiting to come out one at a time? I had to see. I had to go to the place where he had been.

"Can you take me somewhere?"

"Where to?" He got up and stretched.

"The Driftwood Star Motel."

He grinned; then he reached into his pocket for his keys.

Chapter Seventeen

THE DRIFTWOOD STAR LOOKS LIKE A DREAM that's collapsed. It's a string of rooms on the edge of town next to a grain elevator. In front there's a rusty swing set without any seats and a picnic table with three legs.

Reese parked in the dirt out front and we went to the door marked OFFICE.

"Didn't know he had any kin," said the woman at the counter. She looked a lot like Auntie Em in *The Wizard of Oz.*

"It wasn't fun cleaning his room, let me tell you. This is a family place; no drinking's allowed. Believe me, that man didn't go by the rules."

"Can I see it?"

"Whatcha wanta see, hon?"

"His room."

"Ain't nothing there. I cleaned out everything." Still, she reached under the counter and handed me a key hanging on a green plastic card that said 8.

"Go ahead. Look if you want. You'll see a bed, a chair, and a night table." Then she squinted at Reese.

"Like I said, this here's a family place. Make it quick and come on back. You'll have to lean on the door a little, being the wood's swollen from the rain."

We headed back out and walked alongside the building. Most of the numbers were still nailed to the doors and 8 wasn't hard to find. Like the rest, the door was splintered and most of the paint had worn off a long time ago.

Reese pressed against it as he turned the key. Finally the door gave way, and he flipped on the light as we crossed inside.

The room was dark, even with the light on. It smelled old like mildew and worn-out carpet. There was a gold vinyl-covered chair next to the door, a chest of drawers, and a nightstand. That's all there was, except for the bed.

I walked over to it. A painting of a forest with a waterfall and a deer hung over the headboard. The stiff spread was made of a cheap shiny material. I touched it with my fingertips and tried to picture my father lying there, but I couldn't.

Reese waited by the door while I walked into the bathroom. It was a tiny cubicle with a plastic curtain in front of the tub and an old toilet with cigarette burns on the seat. I walked back to the bed and stood at the foot.

This was my father's room. I stood there, not feeling a thing. If there were any hidden memories, they weren't going to come here.

"Ready?" Reese broke the silence.

I opened the closet. There were two empty hangers and a fan with the picture of a funeral home on the front. I walked back to the bed and lifted the bedspread. Nothing.

"I'm ready," I answered. We walked back up to the office and laid the key on the counter.

Auntie Em picked up the key and hung it on a nail behind her; then she slid a shoebox across the counter at me.

"Here's some knickknacks. I found 'em in his room. You did say you was kin, didn't you?"

"Sort of," I mumbled as I shuffled through the box. There were a couple of cigarette lighters, a deck of playing cards, some cheap hat pins, a guitar pick, an old pocketknife, mostly junk you couldn't give away in a garage sale.

I put the lid back on the box and handed it back.

"Just a minute," she said. "There was one other thing that mighta been worth something if it hadn'ta been broke. It was a little wooden bird of some kind, a wren, I think. It was kinda cute."

"Do you still have it?" The bird must have been my mother's, the one she'd lost.

"Naw. Like I said, it was broke. One whole wing was off. It got burned with the trash in the barrel outside. Sorry. People won't buy nothing broke, even at a flea market."

I put my hands in my pockets and said I was ready to go.

"Did you see what you wanted to?" Reese asked on the way out.

I said yes. I'd looked everywhere. Nothing echoed from inside me, but a part of me was broken too. I felt like I could never be put together again.

I climbed into the truck. One thing I knew for sure. I was definitely not moving again. I was not going to New Mexico. I had Roo and school.

"Now where to?"

"Can you take me to the drugstore downtown? I need to buy a bus ticket."

Reese started up the truck and backed up through the gravel.

"You going somewhere?"

"Home," I answered.

"You don't ride the bus much, do you?" Teena asked. She was behind the counter chopping up hard-boiled eggs, and R.J. was running around the store in his cape, a bicycle helmet, and swim goggles. I had asked about a reserved seat next to a window.

"What you do is, you just get on the bus and find a seat. That's it. You don't sit next to any men with white shoes and white belts, or women with big purses in their laps who smile real sweet at you. Both kinds of people will talk nonstop for hours. Find somebody who's asleep or who's reading a paperback. You wanta take a couple of egg salad sandwiches?"

I said I'd be fine. The bus would be coming through town around four A.M. It would stop for about five minutes and then would go on.

"Does your mama know about this?" Teena asked as she counted out the dollar bills I handed her. I'd had them since Christmas.

"I haven't told her yet, but I will. She's moving to New Mexico. She knows I can't go with her."

Superman zoomed from one of the aisles and landed beside us. He kicked one leg straight out into the air and chopped the air with his hands.

"Activate!" he said, freezing into a pose that looked like something between a karate position and a dog raising its leg to a tree.

"Did I transform?" he asked.

"You still have chocolate milk around your mouth," Teena remarked. She rubbed at the edge of his lip with her finger.

He looked disappointed. I knew exactly how he felt. Nothing is ever that easy.

His mother picked him up and kissed him. She looked at me.

"You sure you're gonna go off and leave your mama?"

"It's not because I want to. I have to. Besides, she doesn't care that much. She won't even get out of bed."

Teena wrinkled her eyebrows into a frown and set R.J. back down on the floor.

I picked up my ticket from the counter. "Four A.M., right?"

She nodded and R.J. looked up at me.

"Are you a tooth fairy, Shelf-by?" He grinned at me so that I could see he had one bottom tooth missing.

I looked down at his goggles. "Not me," I said.

"I tried to tell him the truth," Teena said. "Fairies live in Scotland or somewhere. It's the same dang place leprechauns come from. He won't believe me, though. He thinks tooth fairies are regular people."

"Are you still my sister?" He reached up and squeezed my fingers.

"Sure," I said. "But I have to go home. I just came to Red Valley for a visit, not to live."

"Did you have fun at the picnic tomorrow?"

"He means the other day," Teena explained. "Time's just a piece of bubble gum to him. You can blow it up, stretch it, save it for later. It's all the same to him." She squatted down to his level.

"R.J., I'll go over this one more time. Tomorrow comes after today. We haven't done it yet. We already did yesterday. That was, well, yesterday."

"Oh," he said.

I looked down at him. "If I have to leave, you won't be mad, will you?"

"Yes." He frowned, standing with his hands on his hips. "I'll be real mad."

"Maybe Reese could be your big brother."

"Will he bring me a root beer?"

I nudged Reese with my elbow.

"Sure, pardner," Reese answered. "I'll bring you one."

"Teena," I said as we were leaving, "tomorrow sometime, after I'm gone, could you check on my mother?"

She said she would, and we left.

"Have you thought about how you're going to get to the bus at four in the morning?" Reese asked as we climbed back into the truck.

"I'll get my mother's keys and drive the car myself. I'll leave a note or something," I explained.

"You don't have a driver's license, do you?"

Some people can complicate anything.

"The highway patrol around here gets bored," he went on to say. "They'd just love to stop a girl like you and take her in for driving without a license, especially at four in the morning."

"Okay. Can you take me?"

"If you're sure this is what you want to do."

"It's what I have to do."

It was getting late by the time we got back to Aunt Onie's. We sat out in front of the house in the truck. It was totally dark; even the porch light was off.

Reese took off his baseball cap and hooked it on his rearview mirror. We hadn't known each other long, and he was a cowboy. I don't like cowboys. But we'd shared a lot in the last two days. I saw him differently than I did at first.

Statistical research says girls without fathers yearn for intimacy. That's what Roo says. She learned it in Psych I. Those kind of girls crave being held and touched. It seems to me that everybody wants that. The hard part is knowing when to stay and when to let go.

Reese touched my cheek.

It was getting late. I told him goodnight and went into the house.

Chapter Eighteen

IT WAS TWO A.M. I THOUGHT IT WAS AUNT ONIE who stepped up the attic stairs as quietly as a ghost, her voice as whispery as the wind.

I thought I heard her say, "Go to the window, Shelby." I sat up in bed expecting to see her standing beside me in her long flannel nightgown, but no one was there. Slowly, I got up and walked toward the window.

The moon, covered in a thin layer of cloud, hung in a hazy circle. Far out beyond the pine trees the blades of the windmill turned around and around, spinning white in the wind.

When I was little I'd climb into bed with my mother on cloudy nights. She'd read *Goodnight Moon.* Even though I'd heard it a thousand times, I loved the round yellow moon, the red balloon hanging by the curtains, and the little rabbit wearing blue-striped pajamas, his bed close by the rocking chair. I stood there shivering, and I wished I could crawl into my mother's bed again and make everything go backward.

The next thing I knew, my watch alarm was beeping in my ear. I'd fallen back asleep and now it was time to go. Groggily, I slipped into the clothes I'd set out, grabbed my backpack, and quickly went down the stairs to the bathroom, where I brushed my teeth and pulled my hair into a clip.

Outside, Reese sat like a shadow on the running board of his truck. I checked my watch. I was already five minutes late, but I waved at him and signaled that I needed another minute.

I had to give my mother one more chance.

I stood outside her door listening to the fan that whirred next to her bed. Finally, I eased open the door. A green light from the clock gave me just enough light to see her. She was lying on her back, one foot outside the covers.

"Mother?"

She heard me; I know because she lifted her arm and placed it over her forehead, covering her eyes.

"I'm leaving on the bus. I'm moving in with Roo." She tensed her toes, curling them back against her foot.

"Reese is taking me." I paused, watching the fan blow her hair, waiting for something.

"I'm leaving," I repeated. She moved as if she were about to sit up; then she rolled to the edge of the bed and turned her back to me. Finally, she raised her arm as if it were the heaviest thing in the world and waved me away.

I swallowed all my feelings and went outside.

"You backing out?" Reese said when I got to his truck.

"You mean do I still want to elope?" I joked.

He grinned at me. "I have to be back to milk by five." He pulled a watch out of his pocket. "We don't have time for a honeymoon. Well, maybe a quick one."

The sky, which hadn't turned into morning yet, was thick and heavy, cloudier than ever. "Let's go," I said. "I'm already running late."

Reese started the engine of the truck and it made a loud coughing noise. I glanced back at the house. All the lights stayed off.

"We'll make it in time, won't we?" I pressed my hands together in a tight wad.

Reese didn't seem concerned at all. He turned on the headlights and backed slowly into the road. "You'll make it," he said calmly.

We'd gone about half a mile, and I was still feeling worried about getting there on time, about everything, when a jackrabbit darted in front of us. It froze in front of the truck, sitting on its haunches, paralyzed.

Reese tapped the horn. The rabbit's eyes stared into the headlights.

"Sometimes they run right under your wheels. You can't do a thing." He tapped the horn again and revved the engine. I looked at my watch. It was ten minutes before the bus was to arrive downtown.

Finally, the rabbit turned and ran into the dark on the other side of the road.

"Don't worry, Shelby," Reese said, sensing my anxiety. "The bus is always late. You'll make it." He gunned the motor and I gripped the edge of the seat as dirt from the road splattered up around us.

"Your mom know you left?"

I nodded. "She'll be leaving for New Mexico in a couple of days." It was too painful to say that she hadn't even lifted her head off the bed.

A few minutes later, I looked at my watch again. Reese was approaching a yellow light swinging over a street near downtown.

"You're not stopping, are you?" There wasn't a vehicle in sight.

"You'll make it, Shelby," he told me again. We waited. The light turned red, then finally green again. We turned onto Main Street and drove past the clinic and toward the corner where the bus was supposed to be.

The drugstore was dark. Not one person waited on the bench for the bus.

"Do you think it already came? That it left already?" My stomach tightened into a knot.

"I don't think so. This bus comes from Oklahoma City, heading south. It's always late." Reese leaned back in the seat.

I set my wrist on my lap and watched the minutes tick. At fifteen after four, it still hadn't arrived. "I must have missed it."

Reese shook his head. "Nope. It'll be here."

"Maybe I should wait outside."

"So it'll get here faster?" Reese grinned, and I looked out again. A big light blurred in the distance, separating into two as it got closer. The brakes squealed as the bus pulled against the curb across the street from us. I reached behind me for my backpack and opened the door.

"He sees us," Reese said. "He's not going to take off without you." He followed me into the street.

Later, on the bus, I remembered what his flannel collar had felt like on my neck, how his belt buckle had pressed into me as he said goodbye.

Surprisingly, the bus was nearly full.

No one sat next to the window directly behind the driver, but there was a large woman in the aisle seat. She had a reading light attached to a plastic headband and she held a paperback romance in front of her face. She looked perfectly absorbed in what she was doing. I squeezed past her, feeling her large knees scrape into me. She hadn't even looked up from the page.

After I got seated, the driver seemed to be in no hurry. He walked down the aisle to the back, checking the baggage bins and speaking to a few of the riders. Finally, he made his way up to the front, and we pulled out.

He took the long way through town, and I wondered if he was looking for stray passengers, but there weren't any. Nobody but me was leaving Red Valley.

Finally we were back on the highway, the same one my mother and I had driven in on a few days earlier.

"Sun'll be up pretty soon." It was the woman next to me. She slapped her open book down on her thigh. "Out here you can tell the difference. Night is night. Day is day. No mistaking it. In the city it's gray all the time, day and night. Course, down in Dallas, where I come from, they got buildings outlined in green, got a gold ball up in the sky, too. They keep the night lit up down there."

I nodded in agreement, thinking it was going to be a long trip.

"So. Are you coming or going?" the woman asked.

I was about to answer, to say going, but the bus driver was slowing down.

I looked out the window. There was the grain elevator, the silos. We were approaching the abandoned gas station where my mother and I had slept the first night we'd come to Red Valley.

Suddenly, the romance novel slid onto the floor. The woman stood up, pointing excitedly. "Wouldja look at that! What in tarnation's on top of that filling station?"

I looked out. Ahead, in the grayish light of the headlights, something rose into the sky from the top of the station.

"It looks like the Statue of Liberty, don't it?" the woman was saying.

I leaned toward the window. A light flashed on and off in the dark like a lighthouse signal.

Suddenly it became clear.

"Stop!" I yelled at the driver, my heart throbbing. "Stop the bus!"

By then the whole bus was awake, and everyone was looking out the windows.

It was my mother. She was in her bathrobe standing on the roof of the gas station. Frantically she waved a flashlight, flashing it on and off into the sky.

"I have to get off the bus!" I shouted. "Please . . . it's my mother!"

The driver grumbled something about it being against the code, but he must have sensed how desperate I was because he pulled the lever that opened the door, and before I knew it, I was jumping off the bus and running on the edge of the road all the way up to the station.

My mother stood there looking down at me, Aunt Onie's ladder leaning against the roof.

"I'm still not going to New Mexico!" I shouted it, as loud as I could.

She started down the ladder.

"I know," she said when she got to the bottom. She took my face into her hands and said again, "I know."

Later, I heard the whole story, how she'd suddenly realized after I left that there wouldn't be another chance, that she couldn't just lie there, that there wasn't much time and she had to stop me, so that I would know.

"Know what?" I asked.

"Know that I wouldn't ever turn my back on you. Not ever again," she said.

We drove into the country, only this time she took a different turn, away from the direction of Aunt

Onie's house, down the crooked road that led to the cemetery. I knew before we got there what she was going to show me.

She shined the flashlight on a small stone marker. His real name had been Richard, and he hadn't ever been an astronaut, of course.

"I never married him, Shelby, but he was your father."

"Aunt Onie said he'd hurt you. She said he'd done it lots of times."

"I kept hoping, believing things would be different."

"But they never were."

She shook her head. Even in the dark, I could see the pain on her face.

"I didn't want you to know. I was afraid, Shelby. He said if he couldn't have me, no one would. He said he'd find us."

That I understood. It was something you read about in the newspaper every day.

Still, there was one thing.

"You left me alone in the bathtub. He was hitting me. I was crying for you and you turned away." The words were as final as the grave where my mother stood barefoot. Nothing in the world could take away what had happened.

"I've played it over and over in my head a million times." She pushed at a clod of dirt with her toe, remembering. "He'd been drinking. He threatened me if I came any closer. I was terrified, Shelby, that you'd be left alone with him if something happened to me. It was the worst moment of my life." She covered her face with her hands, and I saw that she'd done the best that she could.

We walked toward the gate. Some birds had gathered on the barbed-wire fence around the cemetery. They sat there, like a choir that wasn't ready to sing yet, watching us go out.

When we got outside the gate, I stopped. "There's something else I don't get. The photographs. Why did you go to the trouble of cutting out the faces and hiding them in the cellar?"

She looked at me, startled. "Me? I didn't cut out those faces."

"Then who did?"

"He did. In front of me, with his pocketknife. He thought it would make a difference somehow, persuade me that he was nothing without me, that he'd never be complete."

"He cut out the faces, not you?"

She nodded, wincing at the memory. "It was the only thing I took with me that night, besides you."

"But why? Why would you want them?"

"I kept the pictures . . . as a reminder. Part of him was missing, but I was in the picture too, all of me. I'm a whole person, all by myself, Shelby. I didn't ever want to forget it."

My mother opened the car door and I got in. Aunt Onie would be waking up soon, wondering where we'd gone.

"You could have killed yourself getting up on that roof," I said as we started down the road. "What if it had caved in? And where's your shoes? You could have stepped on a nail or something."

My mother did need me. That much was clear.

She said she hadn't been able to find her shoes. It was the last minute and she had to go.

"Do you promise we're not moving to New Mexico?" I didn't have any more money for a bus ticket, but I'd figure out something.

"I promise," she agreed. "I'll cancel everything, the movers, all that stuff."

"And you'll quit talking about it?"

"About moving there, yes. But I still want to visit, maybe drive out to Ghost Ranch, visit the museum."

When we got back to the house, the sun was coming up, and it was beautiful. The sky around Aunt Onie's house was pale orange, like a dreamsicle. Aunt Onie was sitting in her wood-carving chair on the porch. She waved with her good hand, and I strained forward to see if she was holding a knife. She wasn't.

She was holding a piece of paper in the air, grinning and waving it around.

"I found it, Zoe!" she exclaimed as we got up to the steps. "I woke up real early this morning, and I remembered where it was." She handed the paper to my mother. It was the lost sketch, the one with Georgia O'Keeffe's signature at the bottom.

"What is it?" I asked, looking over her shoulder. It was something flying. That's all I could tell.

"That's exactly what I asked Miss O'Keeffe. What is it?"

"And? What'd she say?"

"She wanted to know how it made me feel. Like an angel, I said. Flying in the sky."

I turned the paper around, examining it from several directions. It did sort of look like a huge bony wing curving into the sky. Then again, it looked a whole lot like one of O'Keeffe's cow pelvises. I handed the paper back to my mother.

For her, of course, it was a sign. A sign of hope, a sign that things would finally be better, a sign that made her run out into the dirt in Aunt Onie's yard and twirl around like heaven.

Later, we went down to the cellar to take down the Christmas tree. We swept up the needles and carried the dried trunk up to burn in the trash barrel. While I watched the fire, my mother packed all the ornaments in a box and brought them into the house.

In a way, it wasn't so bad having a couple of more nights in Red Valley. I got to tell Reese goodbye again, and when we stopped at the drugstore to see Teena and R.J. one last time, Teena gave me the little ceramic toothpick holder that was shaped like a cowboy boot. Superman gave me a big kiss.

Last, we stopped by Annabelle's. I wanted to pick up Hamlet.

"I forgot to tell you about his eyes," Annabelle said, holding him up for me to see. "He's got one blue, one brown. To be brown or to be blue, that is the question!" she joked.

She handed the tiny black ball of fur to me and I looked at his little mixed-up face and fell in love with him.

My mother didn't argue. She gathered up his toys and food and carried them out to the car. It'd be a long drive to his new home, but I'd hold him all the way if he wanted me to.

Finally, we'd said all our goodbyes, to all the cats and everyone, and headed down the highway out of town.

For my mother, Red Valley had been the place she could never come to. It had also been where Aunt Onie had taken her in her arms and rocked her.

I'd packed the half-carved bird Aunt Onie had started for me, her dark blood staining its wing. My mother said it reminded her that you can make something good even out of the worst kind of pain.

When we were almost home and Hamlet was asleep on my lap, purring his little baby purr, I understood. All the moves, time after time, my mother had been trying to protect me.

It was just like *Starlight Night*, the painting my mother projected on the wall the night John D. left. The stars had been there the whole time, in a big gold layer behind the night.

And it dawned on me that it was the same with my mother. She had always loved me.

"So, are you going to put all your calendar pages back up on the wall?" I asked her as we saw the skyline of the city.

"I don't know," she answered. "I was looking at some of Aunt Onie's old books. There's this one by Zora Neale Hurston. It really fascinated me. I was thinking maybe the community college could do a Fun Ed course on her."

I leaned back and rubbed Hamlet behind his ears. It was good to be going home.